D0762386

THICKER THAN WATER

THICKER THAN WATER

JANET MAJERUS

FIVE STAR
A part of Gale, Cengage Learning

GALE
CENGAGE Learning™

Detroit • New York • San Francisco • New Haven, Conn • Waterville, Maine • London

GALE
CENGAGE Learning·

LIBRARY OF CONGRESS CATALOGING-IN-PUBLICATION DATA

Majerus, Janet, 1936–
   Thicker than water / Janet Majerus. — 1st ed.
     p. cm.
   ISBN-13: 978-1-59414-869-9 (hardcover)
   ISBN-10: 1-59414-869-4 (hardcover)
    1. Women authors—Fiction. I. Title.
  PS3563.A38763T47 2010
  813'.54—dc22   2010008532

First Edition. First Printing: July 2010.
Published in 2010 in conjunction with Tekno Books and Ed Gorman.

Printed in the United States of America
1 2 3 4 5 6 7 14 13 12 11 10

For my children
Suzie, David, Julie and Karen
And as always for
Bob

ACKNOWLEDGMENTS

I have to thank my friends and colleagues in the No Coast Writers group in Taos, New Mexico, especially Susan Mihalic who keeps us all on the right track. Their expertise, patience and good humor have been a special gift to me. Also my gratitude to my agent Barbara Braun and my editor Denise Dietz. Thank you all.

CHAPTER 1

"Why won't they let the poor souls rest in peace?" Gil asked, stabbing his fork into his baked potato.

I smiled and moved the broccoli spears from one side of my plate to the other. I couldn't help but fixate on his words, "let the poor souls rest in peace," though I substituted "soles" for "souls."

We'd driven over to Springfield from Riverport for dinner to celebrate the forthcoming publication of my new book, *Emily Says: Of Course Ghosts Get Sunburnt.* My agent assured me it was the best yet in the Emily Says series and would take the children's market by storm.

"Since Mom became president of the Spencer County Genealogical Society, it's been chaos," Gil said. "The dining-room table is buried in old records and books. Forget using it for a meal. And Patricia Fowler has practically moved in with us."

"Maybe Patricia's developed a taste for dead people since she's been married to Sheldon, Jr."

"God, Jessie, that's downright ghoulish. How can you say such a thing?"

"Just warped, I guess. Don't you think living over a mortuary, like she does, might make you a bit preoccupied with death and dying? Speaking of Sheldon, I thought I saw him getting into a car in the parking lot when we arrived. Wonder what he was doing over here."

"Maybe drumming up business."

"Honestly, Gil, that's terrible. And you called me ghoulish. Just seems a bit strange for him to be over here on a week night, especially without Patricia."

Gil didn't bother answering me. He shook his head. He was not to be diverted from his complaints about the genealogy craze.

"It was bad before, but now with the excitement over Fred Kroner's will and the mysterious niece who's supposed to inherit his money, the genealogy buffs are out of control. Are you listening to me, Jessie?" he abruptly asked. "You have that otherworldly look about you."

"Of course, I'm listening to you. I was thinking about soles— you know soles of tap shoes, hiking boots, sneakers—not souls of people. Do they get to rest in peace after they're worn and outgrown?"

"I've given up trying to figure out what goes on in that brain of yours. In fact, I don't think I want to know."

"Sorry."

I looked around the restaurant. Several of the customers were nodding acquaintances, but the rest strangers. Well worth the drive to get some privacy. If we'd stayed in Riverport, a steady parade would have stopped at our table to talk to the Sheriff. This night I did not want to share him with anybody or have anyone reporting back to Aunt Henrietta and Cousin Frank. The joy of small-town living! Would I ever get used to it again? I moved my speculation about "soles" to the back of my mind and caught up with Gil's conversation.

"I'd say a seven-million-dollar estate is enough to get people excited. Murder has been committed for a lot less money."

Gil frowned. "I wish you wouldn't mention murder. That's the last thing we need, but unfortunately you're right. It's probably going to get worse before it gets better. People have been

10

going nuts since the lawyers announced the hundred-thousand-dollar finder's fee for locating that mysterious, missing Johanna. I'd be willing to bet a lot she doesn't exist. I think it's old Fred's last jab at his brothers."

"Could be. Fred Kroner was a strange man. My dad was one of the few in the county who did business with him regularly, and I used to complain when Dad insisted I go with him out to the farm. 'Be nice to him,' my dad would say when I whined. 'He likes you.' I have to admit I got so I kind of liked the old coot, even though he insisted on calling me Missy. Said Jessie was no name for a little girl. He always found a nickel behind my ear and gave it to me before I left."

"I didn't realize you knew Fred Kroner that well," Gil said. "My impression of him was that he was almost a recluse."

"Maybe in later years, but my Dad was back and forth to his place a lot when I was growing up. Dad was the broker for his livestock. Strange, I hadn't thought of Fred Kroner, or any of the Kroners for that matter, in years, not since Dad died. Now every place I go, all people want to talk about is the will and this mysterious niece who seems to have materialized out of thin air."

"Pretty convenient, don't you think?" Gil asked. "I assume the lawyers will do a thorough investigation before they hand over the money."

"I'm sure they will. I was trying to remember how long it had been since I last saw Mr. Kroner. I'm pretty sure it was right after my high school graduation. He had called and asked me to come out to the farm. I was amazed when he gave me some beautiful filigreed silver earrings for a graduation present. Said they'd belonged to his mother, and I should have them, because there were no girls in his family to give them to. That's why I was surprised about this niece."

"Are you sure? He told you there were no girls in the family."

"Yes and he was quite emphatic about it, but that was twenty-four years ago. Lots of things can happen in twenty-four years, including, I guess, the appearance of a niece. I think the lawyers are going to have their hands full, because that finder's fee is going to bring a covey of nieces out of the woods. Did the lawyers make the offer or was it included in the will?"

"I don't know," Gil said. "But you can be sure Fred's brothers or that nephew aren't responsible. It's easier to squeeze blood out of a turnip than get money out of a Kroner."

I agreed. I'd gone to school with the nephew, Floyd. All the Kroners seemed to have a one-sided view of sharing. What's the saying? What's mine is mine and what's yours is mine? That fit the Kroners to a T.

"I hear the brothers threatened to dynamite Fred's grave after the will was read. Wouldn't that have been a sight? Those two old gomers cavorting around the cemetery in a hailstorm of granite chips and Fred fragments?"

Gil smiled. "Your humor escapes me sometimes."

"Aw, come on. Where's your sense of the absurd? Tell me. Do you think it's possible there is some long-lost Kroner female?"

"Like I said, I suspect it's old Fred's last joke on his family. The will says if she doesn't turn up within two years or she's dead, half the estate goes to his nephew Floyd and the other half to some televangelist."

I could barely stifle a groan. "Not creepy Floyd? The bane of my existence in school. I can't believe someone hasn't put out a contract on him by now."

Gil ignored my comment. "If I were the Kroners, I'd be more concerned about the preacher than some mythical female relative."

"Kind of romantic if there is a long-lost Johanna Kroner out there. The will claims she is the great, great granddaughter of Thomas Kroner and the great niece of Fred Kroner, and the only direct female Kroner descendent."

"I'm not sure about romantic, but, Jessie, think about it. Thomas Kroner disappeared from Spencer County in the early 1870s. By now there could be dozens, hundreds, of descendants spread all over the place. Talk about a needle in a haystack. I figure old Fred wanted to let the family sweat for two years. When no Johanna turns up, the money goes off to Floyd and the head of that 'God's Fellowship' group."

Something I'd heard about Fred Kroner and his will kept nagging at me. "Maybe you're right. But I have a feeling old Fred knew what he was doing. He and his brothers hadn't spoken in forty years, but he must have had information or, at least, thought he had that the rest of the family didn't. The family's claim he was senile won't hold up. There's something there, waiting to be found."

Gil stared intently at me across the table.

"What is it?" I demanded.

He reached over and took my hand. "Jessie, promise me something?"

"Depends. You need to be more specific."

"Please don't go poking around in the Kroners' business."

"What on earth are you talking about?"

Gil sighed. "They're a nasty, litigious bunch."

"Don't worry, the Kroners and their millions hold little interest for me. I'm too busy."

The words that had been dammed up inside me were pouring out again. I was already into the first draft for a new book. It was with anticipation, not dread, that I approached my computer each morning. The next *Emily Says* was well on its way, and maybe I would do something with worn-out soles after that.

I could tell he wasn't convinced I meant what I said. However, it was true. The Kroners were of little interest to me beyond idle speculation.

"I'm just curious like everybody else. Thomas Kroner did run off. He may have started another family someplace and the mysterious Johanna could be a descendent of that union. Someone or something convinced old Fred she existed. I can see why the genealogy buffs are all excited."

"Whole world would be better off if people spent as much time on the living as they do on their moldy ancestors."

I started to argue the merits of genealogical research, but decided my reasons would fall on deaf ears. Some people did carry it to fanatical lengths, but what fun to find a king or a president or even a notorious outlaw on the family tree. Suddenly I remembered where I had heard about the will and the finder's fee. My cousin Frank.

"Why are you frowning?" Gil asked. "Something tells me the wheels are starting to roll around your mind. That worries me."

"Honestly, Gil, have a little faith. I know where I heard about the reward. Old Fred set it up."

"I hesitate to ask where you learned this, but you might as well tell me."

"My aunt Henrietta and Frank."

Gil groaned. "What did they have? Fifth-hand information, guaranteed to be accurate?"

"Now, Gil, don't be so judgmental. It was only secondhand, so the chances are good it's almost correct."

"I'm going to regret this," he said and leaned back in his chair, "but go ahead."

"Frank said that Ambose Dietrick told him that Mr. Kroner revised his will a couple of weeks before his death. Ambose's wife, Lydia, kept house for Fred. She said one day she got called into his study to witness his signature on some legal document. Fred had that lawyer of his from Springfield with him."

Now it was my turn to lean back. "Fred must have figured

out he needed an incentive to ensure a real effort was made to find Johanna."

"Seems like you're making a lot of suppositions without much to back them up."

"Not really. There's more. Lydia said at supper that night Fred was in a real talkative mood, which was unusual for him. He told her he was ready to go when his maker called, now that he'd made sure those bastards—she assumed he meant his brothers since the only time he used profanity was when he talked about them—were left out in the cold. He said he had Patricia Fowler to thank."

"What a strange thing to say, but it doesn't prove anything. Wonder what Patricia had to do with it?"

"Who knows? Lydia said he got real quiet after that and didn't say anything more until she brought him his whiskey just before she left. 'I should have looked for her myself,' he told Lydia, 'but it's too late for that. At least the bounty I'm offering is only payable if she's alive. That should protect her.' Lydia said he never mentioned it again, and two weeks later he was dead. Surprised everybody that he went so fast."

"There's an awful lot of 'he said, she said' in this story. I know you spent most of your adult life living in St. Louis, but surely you remember enough about the Spencer County gossip mill not to believe such a multihanded tale. Lord knows what it was originally."

I laughed. "I know, but . . ."

"Jessie, no buts."

"I give up," I said and looked past Gil toward the entrance of the restaurant that came off the lobby of the hotel. A distinguished gray-haired man in a well-cut pinstripe was standing in the doorway, surveying the tables. He looked vaguely familiar, but before I could make any kind of connection, he turned and walked away. Probably come to me in the middle of the night, I thought, and turned my attention back to Gil.

"Anyway, after the weekend, you'll be able to reclaim the dining-room table. At the last Library Board meeting, Florence said she and the staff had the upstairs room cleared so the Genealogical Society could move in."

Gil didn't look convinced. "Knowing my mom, she'll still bring half of it home every night." He stopped and leaned across the table, taking my hand in his. "God you're beautiful, my red-haired darling," giving me a look that caused an eruption of butterflies in my stomach.

I felt myself flush. Forty-two years old and I still blushed like a teenager. But the truth be known, Gil made me feel like a teenager.

I was startled to see Gil suddenly frown.

"Damn that Clarence," he muttered. "I told him not to bother me tonight."

"What are you talking about?" I asked as he drew back his hand, reached under his jacket, and detached his beeper from his belt.

"Excuse me, I better call in."

"I didn't hear any beep. What do you have? Extrasensory perception?"

"I had it on vibrate."

I smiled as I watched him leave the room. Tall and lanky. Tall enough so that even standing at five foot ten as I did, I had to look up to him. I loved to watch him move. He wasn't hand-some in the classic sense, but he had what my mom used to call "presence." Everybody took notice when he came into a room. We were seeing more and more of each other, and I knew tongues were wagging all over town about the Sheriff and the girl who came back home. Esther Benson even asked me the other day if they were going to hear wedding bells soon. Aunt Henrietta put me through a full-scale interrogation every time she found out we had been together. So far I managed it with smiles and noncommittal answers, but my patience was wearing thin. But I knew it wasn't only the nosy Parkers who bothered me, but my own feelings that I was trying to come to grips with.

Before I could reflect further, Gil came hurrying back into the dining room. "Sorry, Jessie," he said. "We've got to go."

"What's wrong?"

"Fred Kroner's house is in flames. Chief says it looks like someone torched the place."

CHAPTER 2

"This is not the way I envisioned the evening ending." Gil unlocked the car door for me. "I'll run you home before I go to Kroner's place. No telling how long I'll be."

It wasn't the way I had envisioned the evening ending either, I thought as I got into the car. So much for romance. But, if I couldn't have him to myself, no way would I let him take me home and miss all the excitement. "Nonsense," I said. "Kroner's is on the way. I'll come with you."

Before Gil could argue the point, his radio crackled to life. I leaned forward, hoping for information, but the conversation was cryptic to the point of absurdity, consisting mostly of grunts and yeahs. Damn, I thought. You'd think he'd at least ask for a few details.

"It's almost twenty hundred hours. I'll be there inside forty-five minutes."

I did a quick calculation and smiled. Good. Forty-five meant he was going directly there. But before I could relish the turn of events, the car roared forward, the pressure pinning my body against the back of the seat.

"Hang on." Gil pulled a light from beneath the dashboard. He attached it to the top of the car with his left hand as he steered in and out of traffic with his right.

My heart pounded as the car continued to accelerate. The red light bounced off the cars that we sped past. I hadn't had a ride like this since I was a teenager, racing on the back roads of

Spencer County. I avoided looking at the speedometer. In a few minutes we were out of town and on the highway. I cleared my throat several times before I spoke, but even with that my voice sounded tinny to my ear.

"You sure know how to show a girl a fun time."

Gil's only reply was a grunt as he flicked on the siren to warn an oblivious driver to move over.

I unclenched my fingers from the chicken strap and tried to relax, reminding myself that Gil knew what he was doing.

"It doesn't make sense. Why would anyone set fire to Fred Kroner's house?"

Gil shrugged his shoulders. "I don't know. A vacant house is always a temptation."

I could tell from his tone of voice that he was not about to engage in idle speculation. Too bad. Half the fun of any situation is bouncing the "what ifs" back and forth with someone. I glanced at my watch. Thirty minutes since we left the restaurant. Before I had time to speculate about how much further it was, we reached the turn-off to Kroner's place. Gil braked slightly and made a sharp right onto the blacktop. My body strained against the shoulder strap as we skidded around the corner.

"Do you think we'll be able to see the flames?" I asked, scanning the horizon ahead.

"Doubtful. The Chief said the roof had already gone by the time the equipment arrived. Probably no more than a smoldering pile by now. Those old frame farmhouses are like tinder boxes."

I stifled a sigh. I knew I harbored a streak of voyeurism, well aware I had been excited at the prospect of watching roaring towers of flame engulfing the house. I had never forgotten the almost sexual rush I had felt as a young woman when the lumberyard in town caught fire, the orange tongues of fire leaping into the sky, resonating through my body.

Off in the distance, red lights were flashing. As we got closer to Kroner's place, I could see Gil was correct. There were no big flames, just columns of smoke disappearing into the dark sky from small isolated piles of burning debris. Here and there sections of wall remained, hinting at the shape of the two-story frame house, almost like a dot-to-dot puzzle waiting to be connected. There didn't look to be much of the house left for whichever party won the inheritance fight—the long-lost niece or the nephew and Reverend Smythe.

Gil skidded to a stop behind Fire Chief Gilmore's car and was out before the car stopped rocking. "Stay here," he yelled as he slammed the door.

Several dozen men, enveloped in turnout gear, were moving like specters around the remains of the house. Some were spraying water on the smoldering piles of rubble while others probed at smoking timbers with iron rods and fire axes. The hoses snaked along the ground. I could hear an engine off to the east of the house, a pump sucking water out of the pond and feeding it to the hoses.

Gil disappeared from sight. The spotlights from the trucks played in what seemed a random fashion over the fire scene. I counted six pieces of equipment, including two pumpers and the ambulance from the Spencer County Volunteer Fire Department. I wondered briefly why they had bothered to bring the ambulance to an empty house, but then realized it was for the safety of the firefighters. It appeared half the cars and pickups in the County were lining the road in front of the house. The people stood in clusters, watching the activity.

I rolled down the window of the car, hoping to pick up some of the conversation, but all I heard were disjointed shouts. Acrid smoke saturated the air. I pulled my silk neck scarf up to cover my nose and wondered how the men working up close could breathe.

The firefighters drifted in and out of the spotlights, encircled with wisps of smoke. The bushes and trees rimming the hollow space where the house had stood were singed and withered. I wondered if this is what Hell looked like. I couldn't remember how the landscape had been configured. I finally caught a glimpse of Gil across the way, walking slowly with the Chief, his head lowered, listening but not watching as Chief Gilmore gestured first one way and then another.

I tried to settle back to wait, but I didn't like the role of observer. I wanted desperately to be in the middle of the action. But before I could dwell on my situation further, a loud crash resounded and billows of debris belched into the air.

I leaned forward to get a better look as a circle of men converged on a spot that, if I remembered correctly, was close to where the side door had been. When I accompanied Dad, I was always shooed out that door, which opened from Mr. Kroner's study onto a screened porch.

"Wait out there, Missy," Mr. Kroner would say. "This is men's talk." And each time I'd stomp my foot and mutter, "My name's not Missy." A warning look from my dad stifled any further objections to being banished.

The screen on the porch had been rusty and ripped in places, and the green steel chairs and the floor gritty with dust. The road was not black topped then, and every time a pickup or car passed, billows of dust washed across the yard and house, painting the landscape with a monochromatic glaze of gray.

Funny the things a person remembers, I thought. My main memory from one of those spring days, after I had gotten over my snit, was lilacs. There had been a huge lilac bush in front of the porch. It was in full bloom and bundles of purple blossoms cascaded over the bush, perfuming the entire yard.

The men finally finished their business and walked out onto the porch.

"That sure is a pretty lilac bush," I said to Mr. Kroner, forgiving him for slighting me, as I always did. "Wish my mom could see it. Lilac's her favorite."

Mr. Kroner had looked at me and then at the lilac bush, surprised, as if he had just become aware of both our existences. He grunted and cleared his throat. "Smells up the whole damn house," he said.

"Yeah, but it's really a nice smell," I said.

His expression changed. I couldn't tell whether it was a grimace or a smile, but I certainly didn't expect what he said. "Tell you what, Missy, let's get an armload of those flowers and you can take them home to that nice mother of yours."

He broke off whole branches and piled them in my arms. Dad finally protested he was stripping the bush, but Mr. Kroner just said, "Hell, Schroeder, might as well go to someone who'll enjoy 'em."

He was an intractable man, and according to Dad, as he aged he got even harder to deal with. By the time I was in high school, I rarely accompanied Dad on his visits, but he always brought back greetings from Mr. Kroner for Missy along with a bag of sugar-sprinkled candy orange slices—vile things that even the dog wouldn't eat.

I could just make out some gnarled sticks poking up right where the porch had ended. Surely that couldn't have been the same lilac bush. The day Mr. Kroner gave me the flowers was thirty years ago. I felt a wave of sadness. I wasn't sure if it was for Mr. Kroner or the lilac bush or myself.

"Chief, Sheriff. Quick. Get some light over here. We found something." The shouts brought me back.

Several men rushed over. I saw Gil push them aside and then his head disappeared. He's either been sucked into the earth or he's kneeling down to look at something, I thought. My curiosity was getting the better of me. Surely no one would notice if I got out of the car. The people up by the road were out of their cars, so why shouldn't I do the same?

I eased the door open and slid out of the seat, the smell more intense than inside the car, and the ground muddy where the firefighters had run their hoses. My heels sank into the muck. I was doing irreparable damage to my black suede pumps, but they were several years old. Besides, I had never particularly liked them.

One of the men had gone to the Chief's car and came back carrying a black case. Gil's head reappeared for a minute. He pushed the people back from the center of the circle. I eased closer, glad that I was wearing my black wool coat instead of my camel's hair, concentrating on not losing a shoe in the mud.

Staccato flashes lit up the landscape. There must have been a camera in the black case. I strained to see what the camera was focusing on, but the flashes blurred rather than defined the target.

"Get a light over here," Gil yelled.

As the spotlight swung toward where Gil was pointing, I squeezed closer to the action. What I saw when the light illuminated the pile of smoking debris brought me to a halt. A charred arm, lifted skyward as if in supplication, fingers clenched.

I must have screamed, because the next thing I knew two men were grabbing my arms and yanking me backward. Gil's voice thundered in my ears. "Get her out of here. Now."

Before I could object or say anything, I found myself back in Gil's car with Deputy Sheriff Clarence Hockmeyer sitting beside me.

"Sorry, Miss Schroeder, didn't mean to man handle you, but this here is a probable crime scene. We got to keep it clear."

I stared at him for a few minutes, trying to bring order to my thoughts before I spoke. "Clarence, tell me I didn't see what I saw."

" 'Fraid you did."

All I could do was stare into the night. A body in the ruins of Fred Kroner's house. Why? And more importantly—who? I watched silently as two men started stringing orange ribbon between the trees that ringed the edge of what remained of the house.

"What's going on, Clarence?"

All he did was shrug.

"Was it an accident? Or maybe . . ." I couldn't finish. Surely not, I thought, not murder.

Clarence shrugged again. "We won't be sure about anything until the arson experts from Springfield come tomorrow and then the forensic people get their turn, but it looks pretty suspicious. When that wall collapsed, we found a big ole safe, but it was too hot to handle. Then the spotlight lit up the scene and we found, you know."

I was aware that my feet were turning into blocks of ice. I wiggled my toes to keep the circulation going and peered at the scene across from me. Gil had moved everyone back. One of the men in fire gear moved around with the camera, taking flash after flash—first standing, then kneeling, from every angle.

I finally kicked off my sodden shoes and bent over to massage my toes, wondering how long it took frostbite to set in. I wished Gil had left the keys in the car so I could start it and turn on the heater. Maybe Clarence would get them for me. It was easier to think about my cold feet than the charred body entombed in the burnt timbers of the old farmhouse.

"Sheriff says for me to take you home. No sense you sitting out here freezing yourself."

"Oh, I don't want to be a bother," I said, though the thought of my warm house was appealing.

"No bother. Nothing left for me to do here. Sheriff wants me back at the office. Think you can make it over to my car?"

I nodded. It took a massive surge of willpower to put my feet back into the soggy suede and slop through the mud to Clarence's patrol car.

By the time we made it back to the highway, the heater was putting out warm air. I slipped off my shoes again. "I'm afraid I've gotten mud all over your floor mat."

"That's not the worst this car has seen." Clarence laughed. "Every time Homer's on duty he manages to spill his coffee and drip catsup and hamburger grease all over everything. They're used to it down at the car wash."

"Do you have any idea who could have done a thing like this?" I asked.

"Nope, too soon. But then those arson boys are pretty sharp." He shook his head. "Beats me how they do it. Sheriff sent Homer and me over to Springfield to the fire academy for a short course. He's big on having the police and fire people sharing information, and he said it'd be good for us to understand what to look for in suspected arson cases."

He shook his head again. " 'Bout the only thing we learned that was worthwhile was the telephone number of the arson unit."

"Do you think it was some vagrant trying to get out of the cold or looking for something to steal?" I asked. "He could have started a fire to keep warm and it got out of hand and trapped him."

"Could be," Clarence said. As opposed to Gil, Clarence was a natural talker and always ready to speculate. "Or it could have been some doper looking for a place to hole up. Wasn't no secret the place was empty. I'm just hoping it wasn't a bunch of local kids. You know how they seek out places to congregate. Could be a group of them came out and things got out of control."

25

"But that wouldn't explain the arson theory," I started to say, then was drowned out by Gil's voice booming out of Clarence's radio.

"Yeah, Sheriff," Clarence answered back.

"How close are you to Miss Schroder's?"

"'Bout five minutes. What's up?"

"Soon as you get her home, call Homer and tell him to go in and cover the office. The Kroners just showed up. I need you back out here. And we got the safe open. It's going to be a long night."

CHAPTER 3

"Yes, sir. This here's a ten three. Over and out."

Ten three? Didn't he mean ten four? And wasn't it truckers who used the ten four, not police officers?

Clarence whistled between his teeth. "I hope those Kroners left their shotguns at home. They are one mean bunch."

"Well, here we are," Clarence said as he stopped the car by my gate.

"Do you mind if I come in and use your phone to call Homer? I could use the radio, but half the time he forgets to turn on the unit he keeps at home. Guess I better call the wife too and tell her I'll be late."

"No problem." I tried to sound as dispassionate as possible, but my scrabbling fingers searching through my purse for the door key gave me away. The horrific scene at the fire had finally sunk in. A body! My God, what is Spencer County coming to? I thought. But who and why?

My steak from dinner rumbled in my stomach as my mind replayed the discovery—the picture permanently imprinted in my mind.

I flicked on the ceiling light and deposited my filthy shoes on the rug by the door. Genevieve unwound herself from the chair where she was curled up and strolled over to give the shoes the once-over. One poke with her nose and she immediately stalked away, flicking her tail back and forth—a cat's ultimate disapproval. That settles it, I thought. Into the trash with the black

27

suede pumps.

"The phone's over there on the wall. I'll leave while you make your calls."

"Whatever for?" Clarence asked, looking at me as if I had taken leave of my senses. "Ain't nothing I know that you don't already know." He stopped. "Begging your pardon, Miss Schroeder, I didn't mean to sound flip. Sheriff would have my hide if he heard me. He's all the time preaching respect for the client—that's what he calls the citizens. Says they're paying the bills and we better never forget it."

"Don't worry about it."

I tried to make myself busy as Clarence made his calls but found all I was accomplishing was moving the canister set into varying geometric patterns on the countertop. His commentary was pretty colorful, but the facts stayed as skeletal as before. Fire at Kroner's. Probably arson. Body. Safe.

"Well, that does it." Clarence hung up the telephone. "Now back to the salt mines."

I watched until Clarence's patrol car pulled out of the driveway, then locked the door, setting the dead bolt that Gil had insisted I install. "You're an open invitation," he had said, "living out here all alone."

I hated the fortress mentality, but it was easier to comply than argue with him, at least on this point. And this night it felt like a good idea.

Genevieve had reclaimed her spot on the chair. I picked her up and moved her to my lap as I stared out into the dark night. The sky was full of stars, but the ground below was pitch black. Even the pole light on the barn seemed to be struggling to maintain its circle of light.

"Probably going to have a hard frost tonight," I said, scratching behind Genevieve's ears to catch her attention and divert mine from the events of the evening.

The start of the cold months always irritated me. I didn't like being cooped up, and even though I stuck to my jogging schedule, my runner's high was tinged with melancholy. Every year I tried to convince myself that winter was a time of rest and rejuvenation, a time to recharge the batteries, but I was never successful. November was the worst; the calendar seemed to stretch endlessly.

I glanced at the clock. I'd missed the ten o'clock news, but that was all right. I'd been exposed to enough mayhem for one day.

I was tired but strangely unwilling to go to bed. Even more peculiar was my reluctance to review the events of the evening. Must be sensory overload, I muttered, but I knew it was more than that. I kept getting stuck on the moment in the restaurant when Gil had reached across the table and taken my hand. Then that damned beeper had gone off.

It wasn't Gil's fault. As he said, "It came with the territory." But tonight, of all nights, I had not planned to share him with anybody.

"Stop feeling sorry for yourself," I said, pushing Genevieve off my lap. A shower, that's what I needed. My hair and clothes reeked of smoke.

I stopped in the bedroom, gathering up my sweats to put on after the shower. Out of the corner of my eye, I saw the walnut jewelry box centered on my dresser that my dad had made for my sixteenth birthday. I lifted the lid and found the delicate silver earrings Mr. Kroner had given me tucked in a corner. I hadn't looked at or worn them in years. When I was younger, I had thought them too old-fashioned.

The hot water coursed over my body and clouds of steam billowed out of the stall. Gradually I relaxed and let my mind work. I seemed to do my best thinking under a watery cascade, and my quarterly water bill reflected how often I needed to retreat to the shower to work through things. This night my thoughts swirled around the conundrum of Fred Kroner's will. I had an awful feeling that things were going to get worse before they got better, though it was difficult to imagine how things could get worse than a body showing up in the ashes of his house.

I rubbed a circle clean on the mirror and peered at myself. Not bad for forty-two. There were a few crinkle lines around my eyes, but on the whole my face was smooth. Gil had called me his "red-haired darling." There were a few gray strands showing up, but my hair was so curly it was not obvious—yet. The decision to dye or not dye did not have to be made for a while. The freckles that were the bane of my existence when I was young had faded as I aged, but a day in the sun made them reappear. I had used gallons of buttermilk when I was a teenager, trying to bleach them. I was fortunate to have inherited my dad's physique not Mom's. I was tall and slender like him. Mom had been short and, as she said, "comfortably plump."

I still found it amazing that I was back in the house I grew up in. After Mom died and my marriage went south, I had abandoned life in St. Louis and crept back to Riverport to start anew among old friends and family.

It was a classic case of running away, and by last summer I was beginning to doubt the wisdom of my move. Small-town living might be idyllic in the abstract, but the reality can be much different, unless a person enjoys residing in a fish bowl. In the beginning I had been so mired in self-pity that I was unaware of the constant scrutiny, especially from Aunt Henrietta and Cousin Frank. How quickly that was changing. I stopped and smiled, enter Gil. And I was writing again. My editor agreed with my agent that the story about the sunburnt ghost was my best ever.

★   ★   ★   ★   ★

Morning came before I was ready for it. The faint odor of smoke clinging to my hair brought back the events of the night before. I was on my second cup of coffee when I heard a car coming up the lane and leaned forward to see a Spencer County sheriff's car stop by the gate. Gil slowly pulled himself out of the driver's seat and walked toward the house.

The acrid smell from the fire entered the kitchen with him, and his forehead was smudged with soot. The lines in his face, which I thought emphasized his ruggedness, this morning only made him look tired.

"Here, let me have your coat. You must be exhausted," I said.

"That coffee sure smells good. Think you could spare a cup?"

He wrapped his hands around the thick mug and inhaled the aroma. He carried his cup over to the table and eased his body into a chair, carefully avoiding the one occupied by Genevieve.

"I'm getting too old for this game. Jeez, it was cold out there."

I had a hundred questions, but I knew in the long run I would find out more if I let him take it at his own pace.

"House is a total loss. If it weren't for the foundation you wouldn't be able to tell it was a house. Neighbor who called in the report said the flames were shooting way into the sky. The arson boys from Springfield showed up at daybreak, but it beats me how they're going to be able to figure anything out. I was pretty impressed that they got there so fast, but they said they were afraid it might rain and wash away important evidence."

I noticed he was looking wistfully into the bottom of his empty mug, and poured him another cup.

"It looked bad last night. Of course, it was hard to tell the magnitude in the dark."

"God, Jessie, I'm so sorry I dragged you out there. Some date I was. And you had to see the, you know, the body."

"No need to apologize," I said.

31

"Then those damned Kroners showed up, ranting and raving and accusing everyone they could think of setting fire to the place. Thought Fred's two brothers were going to have strokes on the spot and that nephew Floyd . . ." Gil shook his head. "He's a real piece of work. Shouting about God's retribution. Good thing Clarence made it back. Took both of us to get him calmed down."

Gil didn't have to tell me Floyd was "a piece of work," I'd had more than my share of run-ins with him when we were in school.

"It's a shame," Gil continued. "The place had gotten pretty run down, but the Fire Chief told me the back section of it was the original farmhouse from about 1850. The Historical Society has been working to get it designated. Plaque out front identified it as one of our century farms. It's amazing how many there are around the county. Farms that have been in the same family and continuously worked for more than a hundred years." He stopped and shook his head again. "Nothing left now but a pile of rubble."

"What about the body? Do you have any idea who it is? And the safe? What about it? Did you find something significant?"

"What do you mean, safe? How'd you find out about that? That's not public information." Gil leveled his eyes at me as if he was about to begin an interrogation, but then he settled back and smiled.

"I forgot. You were still in the car when I radioed Clarence, weren't you?"

I nodded. "I realize you have no obligation to tell me anything, but I thought since I was there, you might be willing to tell me at least a little bit." Even to my ears the words sounded prissy.

Gil's reaction was not what I had expected. He started to laugh. "Jessie Schroeder, if I weren't so darned tired, I'd haul my body out of this chair and come around the table and give you a kiss. No obligation," he started to say, but the laughter choked off the words.

"It's not funny," I said, trying hard to maintain my dignity, but it wasn't working.

"You're right. It's not funny," Gil finally said, wiping his eyes. "What is it you would like to know?"

"Just the facts, sir. But first, let me fix you something to eat. You must be starving."

I got the big cast iron skillet from the cabinet and quickly fried up some bacon and eggs. A proper country woman would have baked biscuits, but in my kitchen he was lucky to get plain toast.

"Now," I said, as he mopped up the last bit of egg on his plate. "Tell me what you know about the body."

Gil stretched out his legs and put his hands behind his head. "Good food. Thank you." He shook his head. "It is probably female, but identification is going to be difficult unless we can get a match from dental records or someone is reported missing. Not much left to identify. If it hadn't been for the hands, we wouldn't have known it was human."

The hands! Hands again! I suppressed a shudder and needed a deep breath before I continued.

"Kind of suspicious that the fire and the body happened right after all the publicity about Fred Kroner's will, don't you think? Makes a person wonder if maybe they have something to do with the inheritance and the missing niece."

"Please, Jessie, let's not go there. As far as we know, this is a simple case of arson, and one of the perpetrators didn't make it out in time."

I settled for a shrug and repeated my question, "Where was the body?"

"In the house, in the west front corner where Fred had his office."

"So the body and the safe were in the same place," I said as casually as I could.

"Yep, fell right out of the . . . ," he stopped. "Do I want to know how you found out where it was?"

"Probably not."

"It was that darned Clarence, wasn't it? I should put a permanent muffler on his mouth. 'Course he was up against the master wheedler. Many a better man would have succumbed."

I decided not to reply to his jibe. "Did you get it open?"

Gil threw up his hands. "I surrender. Yes, we got it open. Soon as it cooled down, I turned the handle and it opened. Someone had been there before us and cleaned it out. Whoever it was hadn't bothered to relock it. At least it saved us an expensive call from the locksmith. 'Course that set the Kroners off again."

Empty! I tried to hide my disappointment. I was sure the safe was going to contain a clue to all the goings-on. Certainly it should have had papers explaining the alleged heiress, Johanna Kroner.

"That's too bad," I said. "Safes aren't supposed to be empty. Not one scrap of paper left?"

Gil looked over my shoulder before he answered. "Pretty much clean as a whistle."

"Wait a minute," I grabbed his arm. "Pretty much clean as a whistle doesn't mean completely clean. Come on, Gil, tell me."

I watched as his brow furrowed and unfurrowed several times, then he shrugged his shoulders and walked slowly over to his coat I had hung by the door. He searched through several pockets before he pulled out a plastic baggie.

"Here," he said, holding it out. "Doesn't mean anything to me, but maybe it will to you. Leave it in the bag. I want to have it dusted for fingerprints."

I took the plastic bag and smoothed it out on the table. Scribbled on the scrap of notebook paper was "Thank you for your donation. 3/10/02. WBG."

CHAPTER 4

"Donation! Fred Kroner never donated anything in his whole life."

Gil smiled. "Maybe not, but someone seems to think he has. What I want to know is, who is WBG?"

The only monograms that came to me immediately were GBS and RLS, which I ran across frequently in crossword puzzles. I tried to remember if I had seen WBG on any towels in the various bathrooms I visited around Spencer County, but came up blank.

"Well, think on it," Gil said. "I'd better get to the office. I sent Clarence home, so Homer's holding down the fort. It's not safe to leave Homer alone too long, or he may start having original thoughts. I'll try to call you later. I still owe you an uninterrupted evening out."

I watched as he turned the car at the head of the lane and headed down to the blacktop. It was almost nine o'clock, but I decided to finish my coffee and clean up the kitchen before I went upstairs to dress for the day. I wasn't due at the library for the Board meeting until one. As I rehashed the information Gil had given me, I couldn't help but think that the fire and the body were somehow tied up with Fred Kroner's will.

Gil had looked tired. 'Course I would too if I'd been up all night. I wondered if he ever regretted his decision to leave Chicago and move back to Riverport. The streets there might have been mean, as he liked to put it, but at least he wasn't on call twenty-four/seven.

I bent over and scooped Genevieve into my lap. "What do you think, cat? Does he regret coming back?"

Genevieve stretched her neck so I could reach her throat and settled into a rhythmic purr as I gently rubbed back and forth. "We hope he doesn't, don't we?"

The wind had fallen off a bit, but the sky remained a dreary gray and the ceiling looked like it was no more than a few feet off the ground. The blossoms on the chrysanthemums were tinged with brown, proof of the heavy frost. I wasn't that crazy about chrysanthemums. The constant pinching and trimming all summer long so they wouldn't bloom too early was a bother. But I kept a few for a last gasp of color. The rest of the garden had been put to sleep for the season, freshly edged and blanketed in thick layers of mulch. It was too early to start planning flowers for spring though I had decided it was time to add more perennials.

"Who in the world . . . ?" The sound of a car in the lane interrupted my thoughts, and I looked out the window to see Aunt Henrietta and Uncle George's Buick pull up to the gate. George got out of the car, hustled around to the passenger side and helped Henrietta out. I had to smile. I suspected Aunt Henrietta would sit there all day rather than open the door for herself.

George and my father had been brothers. My dad was the gregarious one, drawing people in like a pied piper. "Never met a stranger," my mom used to say with an occasional tinge of complaint in her voice, especially after he had handed out the last piece of fried chicken to an uninvited visitor. Uncle George, on the other hand, always stood back, waiting for the dust to settle before he offered his hand.

Aunt Henrietta was the undisputed matriarch of the entire Schroeder clan, a role she relished. I couldn't help loving her,

I'd been in and out of her kitchen as much as my own growing up, but she did drive me crazy at times. She assumed everybody's business was hers to know and comment on. Most of the time I ignored her probes, but lately it had become harder.

George was wearing the windbreaker lined with red plaid wool that I had given him for Christmas last year, his ever-present Funks G Hybrid cap, and bib overalls. Henrietta, on the other hand, was wrapped from her head to her toes, starting with a hat made from some kind of animal hair down to her fur-lined boots. It was her usual outdoor winter outfit, but it always amazed me that she could move, swaddled as she was. And indeed, in the cold weather her gait strongly resembled a penguin's. Every time I saw them together, I had to resist reciting the nursery rhyme of Jack Spratt and his wife.

I couldn't suppress a sigh as I put Genevieve down on the floor. Much as I was fond of my aunt and uncle, this morning I didn't feel like visiting with them, especially since the expression on Henrietta's face led me to suspect that she was on some kind of mission.

"What has you stirring so early?" I asked as I opened the door. "Henrietta, did you hear something on the weather I didn't? You look like you're expecting an Arctic gale," I said, giving her a kiss on the tiny bit of pink cheek that was exposed. "Come on in."

Henrietta did not rise to my teasing, but instead clucked her tongue and shook her head. "Jessie, what are you doing in your bedclothes? What will people think?"

What will people think? Henrietta's question threw me off balance and all I could do was stare at her for a minute. Finally, I gave the sash on my robe a tug and said, "Most people wouldn't give it a second thought." I stopped before I said anything further. The last thing I wanted this morning was a verbal sparring match with Henrietta, particularly before I found out the reason for the visit.

Henrietta turned her face away and sighed. She walked across the room and sat down at the kitchen table. She carefully arranged her purse on the table, drew her gloves off slowly, one finger at a time, and laid them parallel to the purse. Only then did she speak. "George, talk to her," she ordered.

From the expression on his face, I could tell my uncle would rather be any place in the world other than my kitchen at the moment. He snatched the cap off his head and worried the bill with his fingers as he carefully studied the floor around his feet.

"Jessie, I want you to know this wasn't my idea."

I waited patiently for him to continue. George was never one to leap straight into a conversation. There would probably be, at a minimum, a discussion of the weather and a recap of the year's corn yield, field by field, before he got to the crux of the matter. However, this time I was wrong.

"I figure you're a grown woman and what you do is your business and nobody else's, but Henrietta here seems to think different."

All I could do was look from one to the other, thoroughly confused. "Perhaps you should explain what you are talking about," I said, in an effort to keep George moving.

Henrietta let out a sigh so deep her bosom rose and fell like a huge wave, threatening to envelop the tabletop. "How could you do this to the family, Jessie?" she asked with a catch to her voice. "Your poor mother must be rolling over in her grave."

"How could I do what?" I was aware my voice was rising as I tried in vain to think of something I had done to rile Henrietta. "George, will you please tell me what's going on?"

George looked from me to Henrietta and then back again. "Well," he paused and cleared his throat. "Henrietta doesn't think it was fitting for you to let Gil Keller stay over last night."

I was aware that my mouth had dropped open as I tried to

figure out what was going on. I finally took a deep breath and plunged in. "I don't know what you are talking about. Gil did not spend the night. Though I must say, if he had, it certainly is none of your business."

Normally, I would never have said such a thing, but I was being accused of doing something I had decided I wanted to do, but because of that damned fire had been denied me. It wasn't fair.

Henrietta shook her head. "George, will you please explain. Jessie doesn't seem to understand there were witnesses. The proof is in the pudding."

I was so nonplused by this time I was speechless, so I motioned with my hand for him to continue.

"Well, anyway," George looked every which way but at me. "Frank was coming home from the Road Commissioners meeting last night. It ran late because they were opening bids to do the repair work on the McGee Creek Bridge and there was disagreement on the Board as to who should get the contract. Anyway, it was after ten when he drove past your place and there was the patrol car sitting in the lane. He mentioned it when he called this morning. Said he didn't think much of it 'cause he figured you was just getting back from your evening in Springfield. Then it wasn't thirty minutes after Frank and me'd talked when I was driving up to the north pasture to check on the gate and, well, Gil's car was still sitting there."

All I could do at that point was look back and forth between Henrietta and George and shake my head. "Not that I'm sure you deserve it, but why don't you take off your wraps and have a cup of coffee while I separate fact from fiction for you."

I delivered the coffee, pushed the sugar and the cream toward Henrietta, and took my seat between them. "I don't know whether to laugh," I said, "or throw you out of my house for being so insulting. I do have to agree with one thing you said,

Henrietta, this whole thing does reflect badly on the family, at least the part of the family you occupy. Now the facts. In case you hadn't heard, Fred Kroner's house burned down last night."

George nodded. "It was on the news this morning. They're saying it was arson. Terrible thing. People burning down houses for the fun of it."

"George, will you be quiet and let Jessie finish," Henrietta interrupted.

"Not only was the house burned," I continued, "but they found a body, maybe the arsonist but they don't know. Our dinner got cut short when Gil was called about it, so I went to the fire with him. To make a long story short, when it became obvious that he was going to be there most of the night, he had Clarence Hockmeyer bring me home. It was Clarence's patrol car Frank saw in the lane while Clarence came in to call his wife and Homer Munson. Then Clarence left and I went to bed."

Henrietta sniffed. "That's all well and good, but what was Gil's car doing here at seven-thirty this morning?" she asked.

I paused for a minute to steady myself before I answered.

"Again, it's none of your business," I said, "but he stopped by for a cup of coffee on his way from Kroner's to the office. He spent the whole night in the freezing cold at the fire scene while we were all snug in our warm beds. I think he deserved a little consideration. I fixed him some breakfast and then he left."

George rolled his coffee mug around in his hands. Finally, he put the mug on the table with a bang and looked straight at me.

"God, do I feel stupid, Jessie. Barging into your house without a fare thee well. I should have known better. Henrietta, don't you have something to say?"

Apologies did not come easy to Henrietta. And I also knew that she would probably add a caveat to whatever she said.

"I guess we may have overreacted, Jessie, but you've got to remember that we're family. Our only concern is your reputation."

I knew they truly believed it was my reputation they were concerned about and I would never be able to convince them that what really bothered them was the fear that my stains might rub off on them. It wasn't worth an argument.

"I appreciate your concern," I said. "But I'm not a little girl who needs supervision. I'm a grown woman and fully capable of taking care of my own reputation."

Henrietta snorted. "Well, it appears to me that you still have a few things to learn. A lady doesn't entertain a man in her bed clothes. You should have had the decency to excuse yourself and gotten dressed. After all, we're not the only people watching you."

"That's enough," George roared. "We've made big enough fools of ourselves for one day. It's time to leave, Henrietta. Put on your coat—now."

After a rather subdued and mumbled goodbye, Henrietta and George left, and I found myself sitting at the table again alone, Henrietta's last words echoing through my mind: "we're not the only people watching you."

I knew I'd been the subject of speculation and gossip ever since I came back to Riverport and Spencer County. Mom had been sick, dying, and I needed to be with her. I hadn't intended to stay. After all, my life and friends were in St. Louis, had been for almost twenty years. Just because Alec decided he had outgrown our marriage (I never figured out exactly what that meant) was no reason for me to abandon my life there.

Maybe it was inertia or the fear of going back to St. Louis alone or maybe it was the comfort of being close to family, I didn't know, but three years later here I sat. Thomas Wolfe had claimed you can't go home again, but I had and it looked like I was here to stay.

Besides, this thing with Gil was nice, I thought and then laughed out loud. This thing with Gil sounded like something a teenager would say. Well, so what. It was nice and just because the community and family felt an obligation to keep me under surveillance, I certainly was not going to take a vow of chastity.

"Pretty strong words, Jessie," I muttered, knowing full well that discretion was the better part of valor when living in a small town.

CHAPTER 5

My plans to work were for naught. After an hour I gave up and shut down my computer having written one page five times and deleting all five versions. Maybe tomorrow—Emily would have to wait. My head was a jumble: arson, a body, a missing heiress, nosy relatives. All I needed was a plague of locusts to round things out.

I wandered around the kitchen, moving things that didn't need moving and then putting them back again. I finally stopped my roaming and sat down at the kitchen table. I said I was not going to get involved in the Kroner affair. Fine, I wouldn't get involved, but there was nothing preventing me from being intrigued by the mystery. Was there a connection between the provisions of the will and the fire? And the body—who could it be? And WBG? Who was WBG?

Finally, it was time to leave for the Library Board meeting. I couldn't believe that I had let Wilma talk me into serving on the Board. "It's a natural," she had said. "Who better than a real-life author to help shepherd the future of the Spencer County Public Library? Besides, it's not good for you to stay cooped up with your computer all the time. You need to mingle."

So mingle I did. The once a month meetings quickly multiplied. I did grumble but actually enjoyed it, especially the time I spent with Wilma on the Library Board. We went back to second grade together when the Baxters had moved to River-port, and many an hour we'd shared in detention. Then Wilma stayed on and married Ralph Gilmore, and I left for the University and another life.

The wind was coming straight out of the north, and by the time I reached the garage my teeth were chattering. The door squeaked and groaned as I heaved it open. I should get Frank over to grease and balance it.

The flag was down on the mailbox, so I stopped to scoop out a fresh supply of catalogs and bills. As I threw the pile down on the seat beside me, I noticed one rather official-looking, cream-colored envelope. It was from the law firm of Scrugs and Benson and postmarked Springfield. What now, I wondered, as I ripped it open.

> *Dear Ms. Schroeder,*
>
> *As the executors of the estate of Frederick K. Kroner, it is our duty to inform you that you have been left a bequest of Five Hundred Dollars ($500.00) in the will of the late Mr. Kroner. The bequest states that the money is to be used to plant purple lilacs in the location of your choice.*
>
> *Please contact our office at your earliest convenience to discuss the disposition of the bequest.*

The letter was signed Marvin B. Scrugs.

All I could do was sit there and stare at the letter. Five hundred dollars for lilacs!

The longer I looked at the message from the lawyer, the more nervous I became. Damn that Fred Kroner. What had been up until a few moments ago mostly an academic exercise in speculation now had become more personalized. Intellectually I knew that did not have to be the case, but my visceral self was more realistic. That old man had set his hook in Missy.

I slowly pulled my car out onto the blacktop road and turned left toward the center of Riverport. My house and yard were just inside the town limits, an annexation coup engineered by

45

my dad shortly before he died so he could subdivide and sell some of our property. The rest of the farm remained in the county. Profits from the sale had provided a tidy nest egg for Mom and now the interest on the investment made a nice addition to my book royalties.

It took less than ten minutes to get to the library. As usual I was early. I had not adjusted to the short distances and lack of traffic. You've come a long way from city gridlock, I muttered as I got out of the car. The wind caught at my coat. The sun was making a valiant effort to break through the overcast sky, but I was afraid it was a losing battle.

"Hey, Jessie, wait up."

I turned to see Wilma struggling up the sidewalk behind me, juggling an armload of folders.

"Here, let me help," I said, retrieving several that threatened to escape.

"Isn't it terrible what happened at the Kroner place last night?" Wilma said. "Ralph didn't get home till dawn. Frozen to the bone he was. And a body! Ralph said there was no way they could identify who it was." She stopped and shook her head. "And on top of all that, we've lost another of our historic homesteads in the county."

"It was a gruesome scene," I said, reluctant to comment further. "Hold on, I'll get the door for you."

"Ralph said you were there for awhile. Arrived with the Sheriff." Wilma looked sideways at me and grinned.

I gave what I hoped was a nonchalant smile in return. Not Wilma too, I thought. "He said there wasn't a wall left standing. But terrible as it was, we do have to be grateful for small blessings."

"What's that?" I asked, relieved Wilma seemed willing to move on to subjects other than my relationship with Gil.

"Remember that article Herb Springer had in the *Argus* last summer about the Historical Society asking for papers and photographs to use in the book Grace Michaelson and I are putting together to commemorate the 150-year anniversary of the founding of Riverport?"

I nodded.

"Well, Fred Kroner called me the next day. He hemmed and hawed for awhile and then finally said he had some materials I might be interested in. I guess he called me instead of Gil's mom because we're distant cousins by marriage, and he felt he could trust me. To make a long story short, Grace and I high-tailed it out there before he could change his mind and hauled a half dozen cartons out of his house. Lord knows what's in them. We haven't started sorting yet, but at least they are safe."

Suddenly it hit me. WBG! Wilma Baxter Gilmore, immediate past president of the Spencer County Historical Society. The initials on the scrap of paper in Fred Kroner's safe. I should have recognized them immediately. Our senior year in high school, Wilma had covered every smooth surface she could find with her and Ralph's initials, even designing flowery monograms.

"Do you sometimes sign things WBG?"

Wilma laughed. "I guess it's a little pretentious, but sometimes when I'm in a hurry I do."

"Were you in a hurry the day you picked up Mr. Kroner's boxes?"

"Why the second degree, Jessie?" Wilma asked. "Is something wrong?"

"Well, that explains at least one thing," I said. "Gil found a piece of paper signed WBG in Mr. Kroner's safe."

"So what? He wanted a receipt, I suppose for tax purposes, so I gave it to him."

I shook my head. "Sometimes, I think my mind is going. I should have known immediately."

"Honestly, Jessie, do you want to tell me what is going on?"

"When Gil found the receipt, he asked me if I knew anyone with the initials WBG. For the life of me I couldn't think of anyone." I paused. "How long have we known each other, Wilma?"

"Thirty-two, thirty-three years. Since second grade. Why?"

"And who drove us crazy our senior year in high school, scrawling Mrs. Ralph Gilmore, Wilma B. Gilmore, and WBG all over everything she could get her hands on?"

"Well, I was in love," Wilma said. "Matter of fact, still am. What's so important about my receipt?"

"I'm not sure," I said. "All this speculation about Fred Kroner's will and the mystery heiress Johanna and now someone seems to have burned down his house and left a body behind." I shrugged. "Maybe there's something in those boxes that could explain a few things."

Wilma gave me a long look. "Why all the interest? You don't have any connection with the Kroners. You're not going to get yourself involved, are you?"

Why does everybody think I am going to get involved?

"Of course not," I said, making my denial as emphatic as I could. "Besides, I do have a bit of the connection. I used to go to Mr. Kroner's with my dad all the time when I was little. He loved to tease me and call me Missy, because he knew it made me mad. He even gave me a present when I graduated. Don't you remember those earrings that you called hopelessly old-fashioned? They were his mother's. And now I've just found out that he left me money in his will to plant lilacs. I'm curious is all. Is it possible for me to look through the boxes?"

Wilma paused for a minute. "Lilacs? I'm sure there's a story behind that. I don't know if a coincidence or what, but those boxes have sat untouched for four months and now for the second time in a week someone wants to look at them."

"What are you talking about?"

"Well, I got a phone call inquiring if the Historical Society had any information on the Kroner family. I think it was a week ago Monday. I mentioned we had some boxes in storage. The man asked if he could look through them, and I explained he would have to wait until the contents were catalogued. As soon as that was finished, he was welcome to look at them. Then when I asked who was calling, he hung up."

"Did you recognize the voice?"

Wilma shook her head. "No, but I remember thinking that it was formal."

"What do you mean formal?"

"I'm not sure. You know, someone like a teacher or a preacher who is careful to enunciate so no one can misunderstand. Anyway, enough of that. You're welcome to look at them. The only thing I ask is that you keep an inventory of what you find and don't remove anything without noting it."

"That's fair," I said. "Where are they?"

"The Society has a storeroom in the basement of the courthouse. Virginia in the Sheriff's Office has the key. If I remember correctly, I think we put them against the east wall."

As we made our way to the Board Room, I thought about Wilma and the other people in Riverport who were becoming an important part of my life again. I had rarely thought about them the twenty-plus years I lived in St. Louis, but, fortunately for me, none of them seemed to hold that against me.

The seven of us on the Library Board, including Wilma and me, were a curious group. I was the junior member, having been appointed by the new mayor two months earlier. The makeup of the Board was four members from town and three from the county.

Our fearless chair was Peter J. Roberts, a retired magistrate judge. His ram-rod posture and head of white hair made him look like a character out of central casting. It was hard to form an opinion of him as he rarely spoke except to call for a vote. The rest of the time he appeared to be asleep. Cousin Frank said his demeanor in the courtroom had been the same. His nickname on the bench was "Forty Winks" Roberts. Any hearing that went over ten minutes got gaveled to a close. Evidently, the voting public approved of his method, because he was elected to five straight four-year terms. He had brought his gavel with him to the Library Board.

The vice chair was Beatrice (Bea) Ellwood, the sister of our deposed mayor, Bernard Ellwood, appointed while he was still in office. Nepotism seemed more the rule than the exception in Riverport, and generally it was passed off with a shrug. Bea stayed on the Board, even after Bernard was indicted. Aunt Henrietta said that since they had different mothers and were only half brother and sister, it was okay. I was going to ask her to explain that line of reasoning, but thought better of it. Bea was as broad as she was tall, and I had never seen her without a smile on her face.

What can I say about Reva Bearden? Forty years a teacher of rhetoric and American Literature at Spencer County High School and a constant thorn in my side during my junior and senior years. Try as I might, I never seemed able to satisfy her demands completely. It was always an A– with the comment, "Good. I expect better next time." Years later, after I published my first *Emily Says,* I received a note from her with a big A emblazoned above the message "I knew you could do better!" The next time I was in town I stopped by to see her and asked her why she had tormented my young years.

"It wasn't torment," she said. "I watched too many talented young women in our small town be allowed to slide by, as if competing to be the best was something a girl shouldn't do. I was doing my part to make sure you didn't fall into that trap."

Needless to say, we have been great friends from that day forward, though I still had trouble calling her anything but Miss Bearden. I had always wondered why she never married. She had a Katherine Hepburn demeanor, and I suspected when she was younger, many a male student was in love with her.

The only other man on the Board besides the judge was Sheldon Fowler, Jr., part of the Fowler dynasty that had run the local funeral home for generations. He had gone to school with Wilma and me. Even then he seemed to be rehearsing to become a funeral director. He didn't walk, he glided around the halls. His voice was soft and soothing, never raucous and teasing like the other boys. His dress and manner impeccable—shirt tail in and shoes polished. Sheldon never wore sneakers. I often wondered then, still did in fact, what would happen if he ever let go. Maybe his genes made it impossible.

The only spark of rebellion Sheldon had shown was to get married, to an outsider, at that. Many of the townspeople had thought that Sheldon was not the marrying kind. The story went that he had met Patricia at a funeral directors' convention in Des Moines, Iowa. It was unclear if she was a participant or part of the support staff, but evidently she had pursued Sheldon till he succumbed. I had to suppress a desire to laugh every time I imagined what wild and crazy times funeral directors must have at conventions.

They lived in that apartment over the mortuary. I couldn't imagine anything more horrendous. The rumor was that Patricia had a bit of a drinking problem. I might too, if I shared my home with the local stiffs. Gil's mom said she often smelled of liquor and mouthwash when she came over to work on genealogy projects.

Every time I saw Sheldon, I had to resist the temptation to pinch him to make sure he was not artificial. His features were perfect, his skin smooth and rosy, his hair thick and wavy.

Everything a little too good to be true. Like a Ken doll. He rarely smiled or frowned, his face a study in neutrality. He and Patricia were the most silent couple I had ever known—two strangers going through life together. I wanted to ask Sheldon what he was doing in Springfield the night of the fire, but this did not seem the appropriate time.

Rounding out the Board was Allison (Allie) Bowman. Now there was a piece of work! She was another appointee of former Mayor Ellwood. There was little doubt what had impressed the mayor of her qualifications. Allie was of indeterminate age, her hair, skin and body manipulated to the nth degree. Her perfect boobs could have been implanted with concrete, nary a jiggle marred the profile. She had married well, and Booter Bowman kept her on a very expensive pedestal. He could well afford it. Ditzy as she was at times, I couldn't help but like her.

Allie always started her comments with the disclaimer, "Well, I'm not smart and educated like the rest of you, but here's what I think," and then go on immediately to prove her preface false.

Everybody wanted to talk about the fire and the body. Someone, I couldn't remember who, even raised the question of what it would mean if the body was the missing Johanna. That generated a lot of speculation. They wanted every detail from me once they found out I had been there, even the judge put in several questions. Allie wanted to know if I had been with "our good-looking sheriff." There was some speculation about Floyd or the church group having a hand in the disaster since they stood to profit if the mysterious Johanna was dead.

The judge said he was sure that Floyd would not resort to violence even to get hold of millions of dollars. Miss Bearden said it would be more typical of Floyd to cheat and lie to get hold of the money. Sheldon was his usual taciturn self and kept trying to get on with the agenda.

Bea Ellwood said forget Floyd. She thought the police should take a close look at the head of that God's Fellowship group. "All kinds of shenanigans are perpetuated by men hiding under the cloak of God," she said. "Look at what those awful priests have done."

Allie let out an indignant yelp. "That is a terrible thing to say, Bea Ellwood. Why Reverend Smythe is just the kindest, sweetest thing and so handsome. He is consumed with the Spirit. I watch him every Sunday night on television." She turned to Sheldon. "You and Patricia have known him forever. Aren't you on the Fellowship Board? He'd never do a horrible thing like that, would he?"

Before Sheldon could answer, everyone started talking at once, so I didn't get to find out what Allie meant by her questions. I made a mental note to ask her later. Finally, the judge gaveled everybody quiet, and we got down to business.

Then the meeting got bogged down in a discussion about limiting Internet access to children, particularly teenagers. For once I managed to keep my mouth shut, not because I didn't have a strong opinion, but because my mind kept drifting toward the Kroner puzzle. The judge reminded us we would be having several extra meetings this month to deal with budget problems. It was after three before I could escape.

I moved my car to the parking lot behind the courthouse. The Sheriff's Office was in the back, and I had to hurry before Virginia left for the day. I must confess I hoped to see Gil and tell him I had solved the mystery of the initials, but his parking space was empty.

"Hi, Ms. Schroeder." Virginia sat on her perch behind the counter that served as the information desk for both the Sheriff and the Volunteer Fire Department. "Sheriff Keller's not here. He's back out at the Kroner place."

She looked at me and smiled. "Too bad your nice evening out got ruined. Clarence told me he sure felt bad having to interrupt your dinner."

Was there anyone in town who didn't know Gil and I had gone out?

I forced my own smile. "When duty calls, it has to be answered."

"That is a fact. Is there anything I can do for you?"

"Actually there is. Would you have the Sheriff call me? Tell him I know whose initials were on the receipt and what it is all about."

I watched as she wrote out a memo and put it in his message box. "Also, Wilma Gilmore said you could give me the key to the Historical Society's storeroom. There's some material there I need to look through."

Virginia slowly pivoted on her stool and reached into a drawer beneath the counter. "Help yourself," she said, pulling out a large skeletal key that looked like it might be used on a dungeon door. "Be sure to bring the key back cause it's the only one we have. Light's not too good, so you better take this too," handing me a flashlight. "The room's about halfway down the hall. There's a sign on the door."

I made my way down the basement corridor, past a warren of dark little rooms. In years past, some of the rooms had been used as jail cells; fortunately a more humane system prevailed now. Light fixtures, each with a single naked bulb, were attached to the wall, the light barely reaching from one to the next. I was grateful for the flashlight.

The key turned easily in the lock and the door swung open, releasing a wave of musty air. I stuck the key in my pocket after checking that the door stayed unlocked after it closed and stepped back in the hall for a minute to let the fresh air neutralize the air in the room.

A stack of cartons labeled *F. Kroner* was pushed up against the east wall, right where Wilma said they would be. I dragged one out into the middle of the floor. Fortunately, the ceiling light was bright enough to work by. It took several tries to get the cord unknotted. When I pulled up the flaps and looked inside, my heart sank. The packing method seemed to have been take a drawer and dump the contents into the box.

I looked around for something to sit on and finally pulled another carton out to use as a seat. I brushed off the cobwebs and grit as best I could, but finally resigned myself to getting my blue wool slacks filthy. If I had any sense, I would come back another day in jeans.

By the time I got the first box emptied, I was feeling discouraged. All I had found was a mishmash of old newspaper clippings, feed receipts, greeting cards without envelopes, and a stack of old photographs. No one had bothered to identify the people in the photos, but a more dour lot I'd never seen. I suspected some of the old daguerreotypes would be valuable to a collector, but they were worthless to me unless I could find out who the people were. The newspaper clippings were brown and brittle and seemed mostly to be reports from the *Spencer County Argus* of prizes won by the Kroners at the annual Spencer County Fair.

I stood and walked around the room to stretch my legs. The room was twelve paces by twelve paces. I wondered how many prisoners had counted those steps. There were no windows, just a grate in the door covered by a wooden flap that opened on the hall side. A peephole, I supposed, so the jailer could check on the inmates. And there was no key hole on the inside of the door, eliminating the opportunity for an inmate to pick the lock. The stone walls had been painted white. Any graffiti obliterated. I stepped out into the hall and stared back into the room.

What in the hell am I doing here? I thought. None of this Kroner mess is any of my business. So what if I knew the old man. And so what if he had left me money to plant lilacs. Let the professionals handle it. Just lock the room and go home.

Sounded simple enough. Just lock the room and go home. I looked at my watch. Not yet five o'clock. Maybe just one more box, then I'd tell Wilma she'd have to find one of the historical society members to do the rest.

I started on the second box without much enthusiasm. The contents were much the same, but about halfway down I finally found something that got my attention. It was a glossy brochure from "God's Fellowship Ministry," the group named in Mr. Kroner's will.

The pamphlet consisted mostly of testimonials from people who claimed they owed their health and good fortune to the Fellowship and the Rev. John W. Smythe, Jr. On the back was a picture of the reverend himself, resplendent in flowing robes, hands resting on a Bible bound in white leather and embossed in gold leaf. I knew these particulars because the Bible was featured on the inside cover. All persons who contributed $500 or more to further God's work received the Bible along with a study guide to the scriptures written by the reverend. I wondered if Mr. Kroner had paid his $500 and received his Bible bound in white leather.

I personally had little use for these professional evangelists, but obviously many people did. And if the Reverend Smythe had provided some solace to Mr. Kroner, what business was it of mine? I stuck the pamphlet in my pocket. Later, if I had time, I might check out this God's Fellowship group.

I resisted the temptation to close up the carton and leave the rest for someone else, but decided a few more minutes wouldn't kill me. I shuffled through more papers. Nothing interesting. Then at the bottom my fingers encountered a box. I pulled it out into the light and lifted the lid.

There staring up at me was a Bible bound in black leather

with gold gilding around the edges. On the frontispiece was written in spidery print, "To Our Son Frederick on his Confirmation from Mother and Father, April 12, 1912." When I took it out of the box and started to riffle through the pages, several envelopes fell out. Now what, I thought and opened the first.

It was filled with newspaper clippings from the *Spencer County Argus*—all of them about me. My election as president of the senior class and a reprint of the speech I gave as class valedictorian. My four-year scholarship to the University of Illinois and election to Phi Beta Kappa. A picture of me and an account of my wedding to Alex. A report of the publication of my first *Emily Says* book. Mom had been diligent in reporting my accomplishments to the local press, and Mr. Kroner seemed to have been as diligent about clipping them and saving them.

All I could do was sit and stare at them. Dad had said that Mr. Kroner always asked after me. Even reported he had bought my first book. Dad had offered to get me to sign it for him, but he'd said no. The response, if I remembered correctly, was "Hell, Schroeder, why bother, she doesn't remember a grouchy old man like me." The last clipping was Dad's obituary.

I put the clippings carefully back. Oh my God, what am I going to do? That grouchy old man had set yet another hook in his Missy.

CHAPTER 6

A knock and a shout at the door brought me out of my reverie.

"Ms. Schroeder, it's Virginia. I'm leaving now. Thought you'd like to know, Sheriff's back. Just put the flashlight and key in my desk drawer when you finish."

"Thanks, Virginia,"

I looked at my watch. Five o'clock. Time to go home. I put the papers back into the carton, all but the advertisement from God's Fellowship and the envelopes from the Bible, and shoved everything back against the wall. I made a note of what I was taking. The remaining boxes would have to wait for another day. I knew I would be back. My good intentions to let someone else finish the inventory had gone by the wayside. I got the key out of my pocket and carefully locked up.

As I made my way out of the basement, I brushed at my clothes, trying to make myself presentable. Maybe Gil had some more information about the fire and the body.

"Do I want to know what you are doing rummaging around in the Historical Society storeroom?" Gil asked when I stuck my head in his door.

"Probably not," I said, walking into his office and perching on the edge of his desk. "By the way, I have solved the mystery of the initials. They are Wilma Gilmore's. Fred Kroner donated a bunch of papers to the Society and he wanted a receipt."

Gil leaned back in his chair. "And I suppose it was happenstance that you decided to go through those papers this afternoon?"

"Are we being a little sarcastic?"

Gil looked startled at my question and rubbed his forehead before he answered. "Sorry. Lack of sleep is catching up with me. Did you find anything interesting?"

I started to tell him about the pamphlet and the Bible, but had second thoughts. I didn't need another lecture about "don't get involved." Besides I had noticed a Web site printed under the reverend's picture. I wanted to check it out.

"Pretty boring so far. There are a bunch of old pictures, but not a single person is identified. Hopefully, some of the Society members will be able to put names to faces. Anyway, you look like you need a good night's sleep. We'll talk tomorrow." Gil did not seem in a mood to give me any more information about last night, so I leaned over and gave him a quick kiss.

"Sleep well," I said.

"Will do, and remember, I still owe you that uninterrupted evening."

Even though it was only a little after five, it was already dark by the time I started home. Another thing I did not like about the onset of winter. I knew there was precious little in my refrigerator in the way of food, but I didn't feel like stopping. Genevieve and I would figure something out.

The streets were strangely empty. It was like the whole town had gone into hibernation. Everybody but me. As I wended my way home, I pondered Gil and Wilma's admonitions about "involvement." I couldn't help being irritated that I was being treated like a child, as if I couldn't make my own decisions.

A person did have to admit, the whole affair was intriguing. First, the will that insisted there was a long-lost heir and the reward being offered to the finder. Second, Mr. Kroner's obvious involvement with this God's Fellowship Group and the Reverend Smythe. And last but not least, the suspicious fire and the body found in the ruins. Did she, if it were a she, have something to do with the inheritance?

As I pulled past the mailbox and into my lane, I thought about the letter I had received from Mr. Kroner's lawyers. I was touched he had remembered that day from so long ago. And the collection of clippings he had kept in his confirmation Bible. I felt like a web was being spun around me, pulling me into the mystery.

Five hundred dollars for lilacs! I wasn't sure how many lilacs that would buy, but I needed to find an appropriate place for them. Maybe even add a couple of bushes myself. I knew they needed good sun. The library might be a good spot.

Genevieve met me at the door and immediately stalked over to her food bowl. No friendly greeting until I supplied the evening's allotment of kibbles. Genevieve had come with the house I inherited from my mother. So what that I was not particularly fond of cats, there was never a question of whether or not she stayed.

I rummaged around in the refrigerator for myself and finally settled on a bowl of cereal. A good thing about living alone was I could eat whatever I wanted, whenever I wanted. Of course, there was a bad side. I had no one to talk to while I was doing it. Genevieve definitely lacked conversational skills.

I sat at the kitchen table, staring out the window. There was not a star to be seen. I hadn't heard the weather forecast, but it wouldn't surprise me if there were a few snow showers before morning. I continued to gaze to the outside, but my mind was looking elsewhere.

For all my complaining about lack of privacy, I had wondered lately if I'd ever emotionally left Riverport. I had slipped back into the rhythm of small-town life too easily. And I had to admit I enjoyed being a big fish in a small pond. My successes with my children's books were embraced by the whole community.

I was jolted from my reverie by Genevieve's leap into my lap. After eating her fill, she had decided it was time to forgive me. I gently rubbed her neck until she settled into a contented purr while I pondered what to do next. Maybe I'd take a peek at the God's Fellowship Web site. Just looking would not commit me to any kind of involvement.

I lifted Genevieve from my lap and put her on the chair cushion. She gave me a reproachful look and settled back down. I got the pamphlet out of my purse and went over to the office niche I had carved out of the corner of the kitchen. I turned on the computer, typed in godsfellowship.com, and sat back to wait.

I turned the brochure back over and studied the picture of the Reverend Smythe. He looked familiar. And the more I stared at the photo, the more convinced I became that I had seen him before. But where? Then it hit me. The restaurant the night of the fire. The man who had looked in the door from the lobby. God's Fellowship Ministry was located in Evanston. What were both Reverend Smythe and Sheldon Fowler doing in Springfield while Fred Kroner's house was burning down? Allie had said the two men went back a long way and that Sheldon was on the board of God's Fellowship. I needed to talk to Allie.

Suddenly the kitchen was filled with the sound of organ music and the screen fluttered with white doves swooping through a sapphire blue sky and circling above a grassy knoll festooned with white crosses. The music softened and a sonorous voice advised that He had given His only begotten Son so that we could have everlasting life. All we had to do was reach for Jesus' hand.

I watched as the doves faded away and the screen filled with choices: Welcome Home!, Ministries, A Call To Prayer, Sermons, Salvation plus an invitation to join or at least sign in. A fancy logo stretched across the top, anchored at one end by a head shot of the reverend. What would happen if I revealed my identity? Would they come knocking on my door? I wondered how Fred Kroner had gotten involved. Had he been seduced by the television program that was described in the brochure? Or had someone come to his door?

The bigger question was, how could I find out more about God's Fellowship and Reverend Smythe without getting personally involved? Before I could examine the question I had put to myself, the telephone rang. Much as I was tempted to ignore it, I knew if it were somebody in my family, they'd have the militia out if I didn't answer.

I doubted it would be Aunt Henrietta; even she would not have the nerve to call me so soon after our little to-do. Maybe it was Cousin Frank. I actually hoped it was, so I could give him grief for precipitating the confrontation with Henrietta and George. He of all people should have known better.

Frank and I had grown up together, the only children of the two brothers. In many ways we had been closer than siblings. He was two years older than I, but I usually instigated our shenanigans though he accepted more than his share of the blame. He had married young and stayed put, running the family farm while I left to explore the world. And now here we were, living a quarter mile apart like we had for the first eighteen years of my life.

I was wrong on both counts; it was neither Aunt Henrietta nor Frank on the phone, it was Wilma Gilmore.

"Sorry to bother you," she said. "Did you get a start on the boxes from Fred Kroner?"

"Yes," I said. "And so far there's not much of interest except a bunch of old pictures with no one identified. Mostly just junk. It looks more like he was cleaning out drawers than archiving historical material."

Wilma sighed. "I was afraid of that."

"Don't give up yet," I said. "I've only been through two boxes. Who knows, the rest may contain a treasure trove."

"Thought you'd like to know I got another call about them this evening from Floyd Kroner, Fred's nephew."

"Oh my God! What did that jerk want?"

"He demanded that they be returned to the family. Said they were private property, and we had no right to them. I tried to explain that they had been donated by the rightful owner, and they were now the property of the Historical Society."

I interrupted her. "I'll bet he started yelling, threatening you and the Society with law suits and anything else he could think of. He was a total ass in high school. From what I hear he's only gotten worse."

Wilma laughed. "You're right on that one, Jessie. Remember how he reacted when you beat him for class president?"

It was my turn to laugh. "Do I ever. He claimed it was illegal for a girl to be president and tried to get the results thrown out. I don't think he has spoken to me to this day."

"I'd say you should count yourself lucky." Wilma paused. "You don't think he could have a legal claim on those boxes, do you?"

"No way. You gave Mr. Kroner a receipt, and Gil found that receipt in the safe at Mr. Kroner's house. I don't think even Floyd is going to challenge the Sheriff."

"I guess you're right," Wilma said. "I'll let you go now, but I thought you'd like to know Floyd is sniffing around."

After I hung up the phone, I turned and stared at my computer screen, which had cycled into its sleep mode. I walked over and turned it off. I'd had enough of God's Fellowship for one day. I'd decide how to pursue it tomorrow.

A question occurred to me. If Wilma thought I shouldn't get "involved," why was she passing on the information about Floyd Kroner? I also wondered how Floyd had found out about the boxes. In fact, where had the previous caller gotten his information and who was he?

I mixed myself a drink and carried it into the living room where I had my television coyly hidden in an old pie cupboard I had rescued from the shed behind the house. I tried to convince myself to watch something "worthwhile" on PBS but settled on a sitcom. Sometimes it felt good to shut off the mind.

The ringing phone brought me back to reality. As before, I was tempted to ignore it, but rejected the urge and headed to the kitchen. I have to get caller ID, I thought as I picked up the receiver.

"Jessie, how are you? It's been a long time," a voice boomed in my ear. "You're really making a name for yourself. 'Course it doesn't surprise me. Even back in high school, I figured you for the big times."

Who in the hell? But before I could interrupt and inquire, the voice went on.

"Feel bad I haven't gotten in touch before now. Not very neighborly of me. Must say I was surprised to hear you had moved back. Always figured you for a city gal."

"Excuse me," I finally got a word in. "I have no idea who this is."

A noise, I guess it was a laugh, assaulted my ears.

"Of course, you don't know! It's been more than twenty years. I'm not sure that my voice had even changed the last time we talked. It's Floyd."

"Floyd?"

"Your old nemesis, Floyd Kroner."

I was stunned. I could not answer for a minute. Old nemesis, my foot! He had never beaten me at anything in his life. My old pain in the butt was more like it.

Trying to make my voice as normal as possible, I said, "Why, this is a surprise. I was sorry to hear about your uncle's death and then the horrible fire at the old homestead. And a body. How upsetting for the family."

I waited for a response but all I got was silence so I plunged on.

"To what do I deserve this phone call?"

"Now, Jessie, don't hurt my feelings. I'm just calling to catch up and say hello. It's time that we renewed an old friendship, don't you think? Thought we could have lunch."

I found it interesting that he had no comment about the fire or body.

"Forgive me, Floyd, but I am not aware we ever had an old friendship. If I remember correctly, we were always on the opposite of every issue."

I couldn't help myself. You would have thought that after all these years I could forgive and forget, but the sound of his smug voice brought up the bile as if a day hadn't passed since I last saw him.

"Now, Jessie, let's let bygones be bygones."

Maybe he was right, but it would take more than his request to make that happen.

"I heard you're sorting through the boxes Uncle Fred donated to the Historical Society. We are anxious to get the business of his will sorted out and that depends on if we actually do have a long-lost relative. We're looking for all the help we can get. I and my uncles were curious if you'd found anything that might help us out."

"I'll certainly keep that in mind. Thanks for calling," I said, but before I could hang up, Floyd interrupted.

"And, uh, if you find anything that would be of help to us, we certainly are prepared to express our gratitude, if you know what I mean."

Of course, I knew what he meant. "I'll keep that in mind," I said in as steely a voice as I could muster and hung up before he could say more.

CHAPTER 7

As far as I was concerned, Floyd Kroner could go whistle Dixie. No way was I going to assist his family in their search or have lunch with him.

Go whistle Dixie? Where had that come from? Oh my God. I was beginning to sound like Aunt Henrietta.

I couldn't believe Floyd had not commented on the body. It, she, had died a death of agony. Wait a minute, I cautioned myself, how do we know she died in the fire? How long would it take to get the autopsy report? I'd have to figure out a way to find out the results. If I asked Gil, I'd probably be put through another lecture. And I was pretty sure autopsy results were not a matter of public record, at least not right away. Maybe there would be something in the *Spencer County Argus* on Thursday.

The weekly *Argus* recorded the foibles, rites of passage, and successes of the residents of Spencer County and Riverport. The police calls and the Soap Box were the most popular sections of the paper, and I was sure the fire and the body would be the front page story in this edition. If a person wanted to learn any news outside our little corner of the world, he needed to go online and read the *St. Louis Post Dispatch* or the *New York Times.*

I finally quit stomping around the kitchen. Floyd Kroner and the other grasping Kroners were not worth my ire. I was still surprised at the visceral reaction Floyd's call had provoked. However, one thing I had determined out of the conversation was that in the morning I was going to finish sorting the boxes in the storage room. The new *Emily Says* would have to wait.

As I made my way upstairs to bed, I tried to review all the events of the last two days, but my mind kept getting stuck on the blackened arm reaching toward me, out of the ashes, as if beseeching me to help. How would they ever find out who it was? I paused on the second step from the top. Wouldn't it be ironic if the body was that of the long-lost Kroner heiress? I thought. How to prove or disprove it would take some doing.

I looked at the pile of papers and books I had collected from the final boxes of Mr. Kroner's stash. Particularly intriguing was all the reference material about creating family trees and a source list of services and people who would do the work for you, for a fee, of course. I couldn't help but wonder how many of these were nothing more than a scam. There was even a wooden plaque claiming to depict the Kroner family crest.

The items needed to be examined more carefully in the light of day. I stuffed everything into a paper bag I had brought with me and scrawled a note detailing what I was taking. It was time to leave. The dusty gloom of the storeroom was getting to me.

Rather than leave the list in the storeroom, I decided to drop by Wilma's house and give it to her. Maybe she could explain some of the material about genealogy that I had found in the boxes. Besides, I wanted to find out what the Riverport grapevine was saying about the fire and the mysterious body.

The fire and the body had been described in lurid detail on the local morning radio news. I was sure the telephone lines were humming before people had finished their morning coffee. And if anyone was tuned into that hum, it was Wilma.

My desire to indulge in a little gossip and speculation with Wilma was thwarted. There was no answer to my knock. I attached a note to the list, asking her to call me, and slipped it through the mail slot. Nothing left to do but go home and face my computer.

I wandered around the kitchen for awhile and finally sat down at my desk, booted the computer, and sat back to wait. But instead of going directly to my manuscript, I went online and typed in godsfellowship.com.

Once again, I had the organ music and swooping doves, but as the music faded things changed. The sonorous voice intoned, "Welcome back, Jessie. Jesus is waiting to embrace you."

All I could do was stare at the screen. How did it know who I was? I hadn't signed in, even though I had been invited to. And I certainly had not given out my e-mail address. Surely I would have known if I had hit some key that made it possible to identify me. Or was there a system on the Web site that recorded everyone who visited?

I could not suppress the chill that ran through my body. Was this Big Brother reincarnated in the guise of God's Fellowship? I leaned back in my chair as I stared at the greeting. It was obvious that I needed to find out more about the Fellowship's place, if any, in this whole affair.

The lawyers. They had asked me to get in touch with them. Since I was a legatee, maybe that gave me the right to see the entire will. I wanted to learn the provisions that handed the money over to the Reverend Smythe and Floyd, when or if the mysterious heiress could not be found or she was dead.

I exited the site and rummaged around on my desk, looking for the letter that informed me of the bequest. What excuse could I give them for asking to see the whole will?

Stop it, Jessie, I chided myself. Why are you becoming tentative all of a sudden? I pushed back from my desk. Good question.

Was I feeling guilty about sticking my nose into the Kroner

affair? No one had asked me to get involved. Quite the opposite. And five hundred dollars for lilacs hardly qualified me as a major player.

My agent had been nagging me to get busy on a new *Emily Says.* Could it be I was using this whole affair as a diversion to avoid writing? It wouldn't be the first time I had manufactured activities to keep me away from my computer.

I decided to delay answering the questions I had addressed to myself. Instead, I went upstairs and put on my winter running outfit. The skies were overcast, but maybe a run in the frosty air would clear my mind. I had three routes mapped out for myself: three, five, and seven miles. My rationale was that I would have an appropriate route to fit the weather and my mood.

Only one problem, seven miles always seemed too long and three miles too short. The result was that day after day I pounded the same five-mile path. There was an advantage. Over the past two years I had memorized every crack, broken curb, and pothole along the way. I could run the route blindfolded.

I dutifully did my warm-ups, but they did not prepare me for the blast of icy air that hit as I stepped outdoors. I could feel my whole body contract. The temperature must have dropped twenty degrees since I'd arrived home two hours earlier.

The road climbed steadily uphill as soon as I turned out of my lane. My breath was puffing out in clouds by the time I passed Cousin Frank's place, a quarter of a mile beyond mine. I made a mental note to call him when I got home. I still hadn't given him grief for his role in Aunt Henrietta's assault on my character. But more important, I needed to know when his grandchildren were coming out next. Betsy and Joey were the official test audience for my stories. Maybe if I had a deadline, I would settle down to writing and let others worry about the Kroner fiasco.

As my legs pounded along the road, I let my mind drift. The

route was a circle, and I had just reached the halfway point when I heard a car coming up behind me. I moved to the right as far as I could and kept an eye out for debris that could trip me up. I was convinced if all the aluminum beer cans that were tossed out car windows in Spencer County were turned in, they could finance a college education. The car slowed and inched up beside me. Some of the local yahoos took sadistic pleasure in intimidation, and I knew in a facedown, I would be the loser. Just as I was deciding to risk a turned ankle and hop the ditch alongside the road, a whoosh of warm air hit me as the window opened. I glanced over my left shoulder to see Clarence waving at me from the patrol car.

"Hey, Miss Schroeder, did you hear the news?" he yelled as he pulled to a stop.

"What news?" I ran in place to keep the sweat from solidifying and encasing me in a solid corset of ice.

"We know who the body is."

That stopped me in my tracks, and I turned and leaned my elbows on the sill. "Are you serious?"

"Yes, ma'am. We found a purse in the yard. It was pretty badly singed, but the stuff inside was readable. And you'll never guess what the driver's license said."

"I have no idea, but hurry up and tell me, Clarence, I'm freezing."

What he had to say totally took my mind off the temperature, and all I could do was gape at him.

"It said she was that Johanna Kroner who was supposed to get old Mr. Kroner's money. And you'll never guess what else."

He paused again for effect and I waved my hand at him to hurry along. "The driver's license was from Idaho. And you know what else?"

I shook my head. "What else, Clarence?"

"She didn't die in the fire. Someone put a bullet right

between her eyes."

"Oh, my God," was all I could say. I had been hoping against hope that it had been an accident, but the picture in my mind of the beseeching arm had made me fear the worst. Unfortunately, the provision Mr. Kroner wrote into the will had not protected her the way he intended. I needed to talk to the lawyers and find out how this changed the disposition of the will. First thing in the morning, I'd give them a call. No more procrastinating.

"I've got to get moving before I turn into an ice cube," I said. "This really changes things, doesn't it?"

"Yes, ma'am, it sure does. Why don't you let me give you a ride? It's getting awful cold."

Tempting as it was, I turned down the offer. As I pounded the blacktop toward home, I found myself getting angry. What right did they, whoever they were, have to thwart the wishes of an old man? I couldn't suppress a shiver as I considered my next thought. Murder had a way of thwarting most plans. And as soon as I got home, I was going to call Gil.

CHAPTER 8

Of course, Gil wasn't in his office, so I left a message with Virginia for him to call. I barely got the phone hung up when it rang. As soon as I said hello, Wilma's breathless voice demanded, "Have you heard? Oh, my God. Can you believe it? Did you talk to Gil? What did he say?"

"Slow down, Wilma," I managed to get in when she stopped for a breath. "I just found out. Clarence flagged me down during my run. And yes, I can't believe it and no, I haven't talked to Gil."

"What are they going to do about the inheritance now, do you think?"

"I assume it will all come to a grinding halt while they pursue the murder."

Wilma let out a big sigh. "I'm sure you're right. What do you think she was doing in that house?"

"Your guess is as good as mine."

Another sigh. "Call me if you hear anything else. Promise?"

"I'll do my best," I said. "By the way, that cretin Floyd called last night trying to make nicey-nicey."

"What did you say?"

"I made it abundantly clear that there was no way I was going to have a friendly relationship with him."

"Watch out," Wilma said. "He can be really mean. It wouldn't be out of character for him to try to run you off the road with that monster Hummer SUV thing of his."

"Don't worry. I'll call if I find out anything more."

I wasn't even halfway to the stairs on my way to take my shower when the phone rang again. At this rate it will be midnight before I get out of my sweaty clothes, I thought and headed back to the kitchen.

"Hi, Cuz," Frank's voice boomed in my ear. "Heard the news?"

"Yes, I've heard the news, but first I have a bone to pick with you."

"What have I done now?"

"You know what you've done. I'm still trying to remove the scarlet A that Aunt Henrietta affixed to my forehead."

Frank laughed. "From the way I hear it from Dad, you pretty much knocked the wind out of Mom. I don't think anyone has ever called her to task before. I doubt there will be a repeat performance from her. Aside from pursed lips and an occasional *tsk*, I don't think she is going to interfere again."

It was my turn to laugh. "You can't be serious, Frank. Maybe when hell freezes over."

"Yeah, I guess you are right. Anyway, isn't it amazing they found out who the body is already? What do you think she was doing at the house?"

"Pretty convenient that purse just happened to be there," I said. As soon as the words were out of my mouth, I knew the location of the purse was no accident.

"Just one of those lucky breaks, I guess," Frank said. "What do you think this means about the will? Think they'll give the money to Floyd and that preacher and his group?"

"I doubt they can do anything until the crime is solved."

"Guess you're right. Anyway, Mildred wants to know if you'll come over for supper tonight. Been a long time since we've seen you."

"I wouldn't call five days a long time," I said. "We went to church together last Sunday."

"You know what I mean. Sit down and visit time."

I did know what he meant. Since I'd moved back to River-port, as Aunt Henrietta would say, we were "thick as thieves" again.

"Tempting," I said, "but I am way behind in my work. I'm hoping to get the rough draft of my next *Emily Says* underway, so I can try it on Betsy and Joey the next time they come to see you." Secretly, I was also hoping I would hear back from Gil. I didn't want to miss his call.

"Swiss steak smothered in mushrooms and onions, string beans, smashed potatoes, and the finale, apple crumb cake with homemade ice cream."

"Stop it," I groaned. Mildred was renowned around Spencer County for her culinary skills, especially her desserts. It was no wonder Frank was twenty pounds over his fighting weight. The thing that was disgusting was Mildred herself was about as big as a minute.

"You're sure?"

"Unfortunately, I am," I said. "Thank Mildred for me."

"Will do. Oh, by the way, I forgot to mention that Floyd Kroner was talking about you the other day down at the hardware store. He said he felt bad that he'd never gotten around to welcoming you back to Riverport. Claimed you'd been close in high school. Said he thought he'd give you a call. Maybe the two of you could get together. I told him not to count on it, because you were awful busy and preoccupied with your writing."

"As far as I am concerned you could have told him I wouldn't be seen dead with him, because he's an obnoxious son of a bitch."

"Whew! That's a pretty extreme reaction. Is something going on I should know about?" Frank asked. "Has he been giving you trouble?"

"No, Frank, I just don't like the guy. He called earlier and tried to make nice. Seemed amazed I'd give him the brush-off."

"I'd be careful if I was you. He can be a vindictive bastard when he wants. He might take it into his head to run you off the road with that Hummer of his."

Obviously, Floyd made a big impression with his Hummer, I thought. Both Wilma and Frank felt it important to point it out. It was no surprise to me that Floyd chose to drive around town behind the wheel of such a monster. Intimidation had always been important with him, even as a kid.

"I'll be careful," I said. I couldn't very well forget with everyone constantly reminding me, I thought. Oh well, take it in stride, they mean well.

"Gotta run," I said. "Thanks for the invite."

This time I did make it upstairs and into the shower. By the time I finished, the steam was billowing around the bathroom and the mirror was completely fogged up.

I took my towel and scrubbed a circle clear. My curls were plastered against my scalp, but I knew as they dried they would gain volume like a mushroom cloud. I was overdue for a haircut. I carefully massaged moisturizer into the crow's feet forming at the corners of my eyes.

I put on a pair of knit slacks. Tight but not too tight. Running and Pilates helped keep my figure in shape. But probably more important were the tall, skinny genes I inherited from my dad.

As I made my way back downstairs, the word *inherited* came back to me. The body at the fire. How would they prove that she was the long-lost heiress? I wished Gil would call. I was piling up a surplus of questions to ask him. And the purse. I wondered if Gil had a theory about its discovery.

I laughed to myself over that speculation. I was sure Gil had a theory, but getting him to share it was problematic. No one could accuse our sheriff of having loose lips.

I finally decided that a watched phone was never going to ring, so I mixed myself a martini to drink while I watched the news. I had switched from gin and tonics on Labor Day. Some people only wore white shoes between Memorial Day and Labor Day. For me, that was the time I drank gin and tonics.

Genevieve jumped up on the sofa next to me and created a nest for herself in my lap. Together we watched the mayhem that seemed to be spreading to all parts of the world. With the advent of the ever-present television news programs, the isolation and innocence that Riverport and other small towns used to enjoy were now a thing of the past.

Finally, the news and my martini were finished, and I headed back to the kitchen. During the numerous commercials, I had decided to fix scrambled eggs with mushrooms and a salad for my dinner. Maybe that would assuage some of the depression that always enveloped me after the broadcast anchors concluded their reports.

Genevieve insisted that I fill up her bowl first. I knew better than to try and put her off. If I did, she would circle my legs, pausing only to nip at my calves with each round, launching me into something resembling a St. Vitas dance.

Just as I was sitting down to eat, the phone rang. Never failed. However, it did not occur to me to ignore it. I was hoping it was Gil. For once, I was correct.

"You called?" was how he started the conversation. No "Hi, Honey" or "Sorry I haven't called sooner." I wondered, did that mean the courting phase was over?

I decided not to make an issue of it. "Yes, I called. Probably one of hundreds, right?"

"God damn that Clarence. He must have spent the whole afternoon driving around Spencer County spreading the word.

There are times I am tempted to get one of those iron chastity belts the knights used for their ladies during the Crusades, only I'd modify it for his mouth."

"How about a mask like they put on Hannibal Lecter?" I countered.

"I doubt if either'd do any good," Gil said. "He'd probably learn sign language or start carrying a chalkboard."

"So, you want to tell me about it?"

"Might as well."

I waited in silence while he sorted through his thoughts. I knew from times past that I'd find out more if I let him take his own sweet time. One of the hardest things I'd had to learn since I moved back to Riverport was patience.

"I guess you know we found a purse."

"Yes, Clarence told me."

"And I guess you know that the driver's license said the purse belonged to a Johanna Kroner from Boise, Idaho."

"I knew Idaho. I didn't know Boise."

"Yeah, Boise."

"What else was in the purse?"

"Not much."

This had gone on long enough. "Honestly, Gil, getting details out of you is as difficult as extracting an impacted wisdom tooth and just about as painful."

Gil laughed. "You wouldn't want me to deprive you of the fun of interrogation, would you?"

It was one of those gotcha moments, and I had to admit that Gil had won this round. "Okay, I concede. Now will you give me the details?"

"As I said, not much. The usual female paraphernalia. One of those compact things you use to put color on your cheeks, lipstick, something called cover-up, also a box of tic tacs, a brush, a ten-dollar bill and a couple of ones, a debit card, and a plastic change purse. That's about it."

"What information's on the driver's license?"

"Says she was born in 1971 which makes her thirty-five, five foot five, one hundred forty pounds, blue eyes, an address in Boise, and no restrictions."

"What does she look like?"

"Either she was an albino or well acquainted with a bleach bottle. Her hair is stark white and her makeup looks like she was ready for a night out on the town."

"Pretty?"

"I'd say it depends on your taste."

"How about your taste?' I asked.

"Not my type. Looks a little shopworn."

"Have you checked on the address in Boise?"

"Jessie, how long have I been in law enforcement?" He paused for emphasis, and I was smart enough to shut my mouth.

"Of course I checked with Boise. A woman named Johanna Kroner, matching her description, had a furnished studio apartment at the address on the license, one of those places that rents by the week. The manager didn't have much to say about her except she kept to herself, no visitors to speak of, and she paid her rent on time. Didn't seem to have a regular job. She lived there a couple of months. Gave notice several weeks ago and cleared out. Police in Boise have no record on her."

"Not much to go on, is there?"

"Not yet. We'll see what comes tomorrow. I gotta go."

"Wait a minute. Was there any kind of paper, lists, receipts, anything like that? An address book?" I was trying to remember what all was stuffed in my various purses.

"Couple of tissues, but that's it."

"What did the purse look like?"

"Medium size. No where near as big as that suitcase you lug around, looked like leather but probably imitation. Had a key chain with a tag that has Coach written on it, whatever that means, but no keys. Listen, honey, I really have to go. I'll call you tomorrow."

With that he abruptly hung up.

Whatever that means! I'll tell you what it means, my darling. It means she paid $300 to $500 for that purse new, and even from a used goods store, it would have been pricey. I doubted it was imitation. The question was, was she?

CHAPTER 9

The day dawned bright and crisp, and I vowed this day I was going to make significant progress on my new *Emily Says*. I also vowed that I would step aside and let the authorities (i.e., Gil) worry about the Kroner mess. I was working on a modification in my storyline and a new title. That was more than enough to keep me busy.

I turned on my computer and checked for E-mail messages. A long one from my friend Ellen detailing the latest St. Louis gossip along with her interpretations. "Saw your ex at the symphony Wednesday with you-know-who," she said. "He's not aging very gracefully. Got him a little pot belly. Never thought I would say this, Jessie, but he did you a big favor. You're sounding better than you have in years."

Ellen was correct, as usual. I was feeling better, but I still couldn't help the twinge that came whenever I heard about Alec. It's not easy to erase twenty years. In fact, I wasn't sure I wanted to. Most of the anger had subsided, and I had abandoned the personal query of "What if I had done something different?" Why do the aggrieved often feel culpable? Good question, I thought, but I wasn't ready to answer that now. Time to get to work.

Before I settled down with Emily and her latest adventure, I decided to call the lawyers. I shuffled through the papers on my desk. I found the letter and quickly dialed the number.

When I asked for Mr. Scrugs and explained the call was about the Kroner Estate, the secretary let out such a sigh it nearly blew my eardrum.

"I'm sorry, but he is unavailable. All queries about the Kroner Estate need to go through our public relations department," she said and promptly hung up, leaving me with nothing but the dial tone for my effort.

My, my, I thought. I guess I'm not the only one curious about what happens to the money.

I hit redial. While I waited for the secretary to answer, I pondered her earlier response. Public relations department? That was a new one! A law firm employing a PR firm. Never occurred to me that lawyers needed more double-speak than they already had.

This time when the secretary came on, I was ready for her. "This is Jessie Schroeder. I am one of the legatees of the Kroner estate. Mr. Scrugs requested that I call him."

After a little sputtering and a lukewarm apology, she put me through to him.

"Miss Schroeder," he said. "As you might suspect, we're at a bit of a standstill on the disposition of Mr. Kroner's estate."

"I assumed as much," I said. "I wondered what requirements must be satisfied before the funds can be released." I'm sure he thought I was rather weird to be concerned about my $500 lilac bequest. If he did, he was careful not to let on.

"The will states that the bulk of the estate is to go to Johanna Kroner. However, if Johanna Kroner is not found within two years or is proven to be deceased, then and only then can the estate be released to the secondary beneficiaries and probate concluded."

He paused. "I guess you know about the body."

"Yes" was all I said and did not go into the gory details of being present when it was discovered.

"We have to wait for the authorities to conclude their

investigation before we can proceed. We will notify you as soon as there has been a decision. Now is there anything else I can do for you today?"

"Is there any way to find out who the other legatees are?"

"Haven't you received a copy of the will?"

"No. All I got was a letter from your office saying that Mr. Kroner had left me a small bequest."

"Oh, dear. As a legatee you should have received a copy of the entire will. I will instruct my secretary to get one out to you as soon as possible. It will probably take a week or so. Call me if you have any questions after you receive it."

"Thank you, I will," I said. The conversation had finally turned interesting.

My computer screen had cycled into its sleep mode while I talked to the lawyer. Before I activated it, I decided to walk down to the mailbox and get the newspaper that was delivered every Thursday. I wondered what Herb Springer and the *Spencer County Argus* would have to say about the whole affair.

It was still bitter cold, but at least the sun was shining. The grass along the side of the lane was crisp with frost. I would wait till later to take my run. As I looked across the road at the woods beyond, I realized it had been at least a month since I had been over there.

I hadn't even gone to gather black walnuts from the tree that towered over the clearing and the little stone house that had been the original structure built by my ancestors in the mid-1800s. The squirrels and chipmunks could have the full harvest this fall. Besides, black walnuts were almost impossible to shell.

Opening them was so difficult that Cousin Frank put them in a gunny sack and ran over them with his truck to rub off the hulls and crack the shells. Then Mildred would sit for hours at the kitchen table and pick at the fractured nuts, slowly collecting a pile of the tangy meats. Her black walnut refrigerator cookies were legend.

I walked across the road and pulled the *Spencer County Argus* from its bright red tube stuck in the ground next to the mailbox and added it to my daily pile of catalogs. As I expected, the fire and body at the Kroner farm were the headline stories. I hurried back to the house so I could read them at my leisure in the warmth of the kitchen.

Herb Springer, the editor, had made generous use of his thesaurus in describing the conflagration, but I didn't learn any new details. He said identification of the body was pending and made no mention of the contents of the purse other than to say it contained personal effects. He quoted Gil who said the investigation was still in the preliminary stage.

Hmmm, I thought, sounds like Gil isn't accepting the driver's license at face value.

I had no idea when I would be talking to Gil, but I knew he would call when he had a chance. It was no longer a question of if, but when. Gone were the days of waiting and wondering. I settled back to finish reading the paper. Emily could wait again.

There were several photos of the burned-out farmhouse. In the moonlight, the scene had looked and felt almost ethereal. Now it just looked sad. Another victim.

I moved on to the rest of the paper. Nothing of interest in the Soap Box. Several of the regular contributors beating their same horses. The calendar of coming events also had nothing of interest. Everybody seemed to be in a holding pattern for November. Finally, there was nothing left but the religion page, a section I normally skipped. I decided to give it a quick glance and then get to work.

It was the birds that caught my eye. There in the lower right corner of the page was a three-column announcement, festooned in doves, that the founder of God's Fellowship, the Rev. John A. Smythe, Jr., would, for one night only, have a public prayer service and private reception at the Abundant Life Church in Riverport. Seating would be limited. Groups wanting a private session with Reverend Smythe were advised to contact Floyd Kroner for additional information.

That knocked me back on my heels. Floyd Kroner working with God's Fellowship! Wasn't that interesting? I wondered how long the relationship had been in existence. Was it long term or a new partnership that had been forged after they were thrown together by the specifications of the will? Somehow I could not see Floyd involved in God's work unless it turned a profit for him. I doubted he had undergone a metamorphosis since high school. I hadn't heard anyone describe him as having mellowed, in fact, quite the opposite.

I pushed myself back from the table, leaving the paper opened to the advertisement for the prayer meeting. It was scheduled for seven P.M. Sunday. I wondered if I should attend. It would be interesting to see the reverend in action. I also wondered if I had been too hasty in turning down Floyd's overtures. I was not quite sure why I had lashed out at him so vehemently. Maybe lunch with him wasn't such a bad idea, though I didn't think I'd be able to work up much of an appetite. It could be he had changed a bit for the better, a possibility I didn't hold out much hope for, but stranger things had happened.

Floyd had been particularly odious in his younger years. His behavior all through school was that of the little boy who wanted desperately to play with the big kids, but didn't know how to pull it off, so he ended up offending everybody.

I pulled out the Riverport and Spencer County telephone book. Maybe I'd just give him a call.

Before I dialed the last digit of his number, I cut the connection. What in the hell did I think I was doing? What did I think I would prove by spending time with the person who had plagued my growing-up years?

I put the hand piece back in the cradle. This was getting me nowhere. Might as well take my run. Maybe that would help me focus, and I could get some writing done. By the time I got my winter gear on, I was sweating. Once outside I would cool off fast, then heat up again. Frank claimed I looked like something from outer space when I got all my Spandex on.

By the time I passed Frank and Mildred's place, I had hit my pace. The ruts along the edge of the road were filled with crusts of icy puddles, so I stayed on the blacktop. I always ran against traffic along this section of road, the curves and hills making visibility difficult. I didn't need one of the natives adding me to the assorted roadkill that littered the verge.

I was not having much luck focusing my mind on Emily and her tale. I knew good and well what part of the problem was. It was more fun to puzzle out an existing mystery than to sit in front of a blank computer screen and try to wrench a fresh story from my imagination. I was also aware that I was going to have to come up with a deadline for myself, one that would bring embarrassment if I did not meet it. It was at times like this that I wondered what on earth had made me take up writing fiction as a profession, especially fiction for children.

The interesting thing was that I knew where I wanted to take Emily. The story was almost fully formed in my head. It was my fingers that I had trouble with. Every time I tried to set them working on the keyboard, they balked.

Ah, well, enjoy the scenery. It will all work out eventually.

This part of Spencer County was beautiful. It was close enough to the river that the streams that made their way into the Mississippi River had cut the land into hills and valleys. Heavy stands of timber, a few surviving first growths, crept up to the sides of the road. All the trees were bare except the oaks, which would not drop their gold and tan leaves until springtime when they would be pushed off to make room for the new. Here and there the timber had been cleared. The fields that had been carved out lay fallow, resting until the next growing season. It must have rained last night because ice crystals coated the stalks of grass. At times like this, I knew I had made the right decision to come back to Riverport.

The sound of an approaching motor jerked me out of my reverie, and I looked ahead to see a gray tank-like machine heading toward me. The windows were tinted, so I couldn't see who or how many people were inside. I wondered if there was some kind of military operation going on I did not know about. Then it hit me. Floyd's Hummer! The one everyone kept warning me about. I jumped the ditch and was halfway over the fence when it came to a stop. The window closest to me slowly slid open.

"My, my, if it isn't our famous author. No need to run away."

There he sat. Older but with the same smirk that seemed to have been etched on his face from birth. Floyd Kroner.

"Hey there, Floyd." I attempted a nonchalant response, but it sounded phony even to my ears. "How's it going?"

"Fair to middling, but I'm still feeling poorly about your refusing to have lunch with me."

I tried to laugh, but it came out more like a grunt. "I'm afraid you caught me at a bad time."

"Yeah. That's what your cousin Frank said. Something about temperamental artists. You always were a bit that way."

I decided not to respond.

"How's about I give you a ride home? It's mighty cold out here."

"Thanks, but I need the exercise. And listen, I'm sorry I was so brusque the other day."

"Well, I'll forgive you, if we can have that lunch. Next Wednesday, noon, at the Uptown Bistro. My treat."

He obviously took my stunned silence as agreement. He

shouted, "See you then," as the window slid closed, erasing his smirk inch by inch.

CHAPTER 10

"You what? You agreed to have lunch with Floyd Kroner? In public! Are you crazy? And at the Uptown Bistro. Everyone in Riverport will see you or know about it within ten minutes."

Wilma was beside herself.

"And what will Gil think?"

The question stopped me in my tracks. What will Gil think? Why should that make a difference?

"Well?" Wilma continued. "And don't look at me like I am some addled-brained ninny. You seem to forget that everything you do is examined under a magnifying glass. And now that you and our bachelor sheriff are an item, it makes it doubly so. What you do reflects on him, and he's up for reelection next spring."

"Wilma, I can't believe what you are saying. Listen to yourself! Besides, he's a widower not a bachelor."

After I finished my run and showered, I had stopped by Wilma's on my way to the supermarket. I had expected sympathy, not a lecture from her.

"Look, it's not until next week. And it's just lunch. I'm not planning to sleep with the jerk. Look at it this way. I'm doing the people of Riverport a favor. They need something to gossip about. November's a pretty slow month."

"All right, maybe I overreacted," she said, "but I still think it's a bad idea."

I had originally thought I would try to con Wilma into going to Reverend Smythe's performance with me on Sunday night. After her eruption about Floyd, I figured that request would bring another lecture, so I said nothing about it and took my leave.

Grocery shopping was one of my least favorite activities, but my cupboards were so bare I was close to begging Genevieve to share her kibbles with me. In St. Louis I had my supermarket aisles memorized, and I could complete my shopping in thirty minutes from car door to car door. In Riverport it was a little different. I had the layout down pat, but at every turn it seemed I ran into someone who wanted to chat. And the simplest query at the butcher counter could provoke a discourse to rival anything heard at the UN.

When I pulled into the parking lot, I saw Floyd's monster car ahead of me, sticking halfway out of a parking space, its backup lights on. The last thing I wanted was another encounter with Floyd, so I turned right, even though the arrows showed I was going the wrong way.

As I maneuvered into a space two rows away from Floyd, I heard the throaty growl of his engine as he stepped on the gas. A movement to the side of his vehicle caught my eye, and I found myself staring at Patricia Fowler, flattened against the car next to where Floyd had been parked. She didn't move until the Hummer roared out of the lot, narrowly missing another car that skidded to a halt in a screech of brakes.

I jumped out of my car and ran over to Patricia. "Are you all right?" I asked.

She nodded and nervously brushed her hair away from her face.

"I thought for a minute he had hit you. What was he thinking of?"

Patricia cleared her throat. "No problem. It was just Floyd being Floyd," she said. "You know how he is with that big car of his, like a teenager showing off."

"More like an idiot, if you ask me," I said.

Patricia didn't agree or disagree with me and after a few seconds she said, "He'll get his someday."

Before I could ask her what she meant, she continued, "Well, I best be going. I need to get Sheldon's dinner on early, because we have a showing tonight."

A showing, I thought, makes it sound more like a movie premiere than a laying out.

I watched as Patricia walked over to her car. What in the world had been going on between her and Floyd?

I made it through the supermarket with minimal interruptions. Even the meat counter went smoothly, though the butcher was eager to rehash the fire and the mysterious body and get my take on the whole affair. I managed to answer most of his questions with monosyllables.

I finally arrived home a little before five o'clock. My answering machine was blinking with two messages. I figured one was from either Aunt Henrietta or Frank. I could count on at least one a day from those two. I hoped the other was from Gil, since he was the reason I had broken down several months before and gotten the machine.

The machine was set to record a message of no more than a minute. Aunt Henrietta had never been able to finish a message in that amount of time and was continually complaining to me about it. Gil, on the other hand, had yet to use up his allotment.

The first was from Frank, telling me that his grandkids, Betsy and Joey, would be coming to stay with him and Mildred the following weekend. "They said to ask you if you would have a new Emily story to tell them," Frank said.

Well, that settled one thing for me. Betsy and Joey were my

frontline critics. I had to get busy. No more avoiding the computer.

The second was from Gil. All I could do was shake my head as I listened. "I hear I have some heavy competition," he said. "Lunch with Floyd. My, my! Call me."

How in the world had Gil found out about the lunch? I was aware news spread fast in Riverport, but this almost set a record. It had been only three hours since I ran into Floyd, and I had told only one person—Wilma. Wilma! How could she! She must have called her husband Ralph. The fire personnel shared the office with the Sheriff's Department. Ralph told Gil.

I couldn't tell from Gil's tone of voice if he was teasing or irritated. No sooner had that reaction hit me than I was irritated myself. What did it matter? I certainly was entitled to have lunch with whomever I pleased.

I hit speed dial for the Sheriff's nonemergency number. Virginia, with her normal efficiency, picked up the phone immediately. "Spencer County Sheriff's Department. How may I direct your call?"

"Hi, Virginia. It's Jessie Schroeder. Is the man in?"

"Well, hi there, Ms. Schroeder. How're you doing?"

"Fine, thank you. Is the Sheriff in?" Sometimes Virginia had to be reminded who the call was for. She inclined toward extracurricular conversation.

"Yes, he was pacing around here just a few minutes ago. Let me put you through."

His greeting was a curt "Sheriff."

"Aren't you Mr. Sunshine? Surely things can't be that bad."

"Yes, they can, and I guarantee they'll get worse. This damn case is driving me nuts. And to make matters worse, just about everybody in town has a theory that he feels he has to share with me."

"I guess this isn't a good time to call," I said. Gil's outburst surprised me. He was usually calm and even tempered. It did occur to me that maybe he was starting to feel so comfortable with me that he was letting me see behind the facade.

"Sorry," Gil said. "It's been one of those days."

"No need to apologize. Want to talk about it? I'll sweeten the deal with dinner, soft music, candlelight, and a nice bottle of wine."

"If only I could," he said. "This whole thing is getting more and more complicated. I'm stuck here waiting for the final report from the arson boys. They promised me they'd have the detailed results today and go over them with me."

"What did the preliminary report say?" I asked.

"You know I can't discuss an ongoing investigation with you, Jessie."

"Come on, Gil. I'm not asking for any more information than you'll give to Herb Springer for the newspaper. Besides, who would I tell?"

"It's not that I worry you will tell. It's that I worry you might decide to start your own detecting. I have a feeling there are some very bad people mixed up in this."

I let the silence grow between us. I figured if I kept quiet long enough he would say something.

"Aren't you going to argue with me?" he said.

"What's the sense in arguing. If you've made up your mind, that's that. I know to accept your decision."

"What am I going to do with you? Have you ever considered applying to the FBI or the CIA for a job as an interrogator, Jessie? They'd hire you in a heartbeat."

"Can I use you as a reference?"

Gil let out a groan. "Look, all the investigators have said up to now is that it definitely was a professional job, not a bunch of kids dousing the place with a can of gasoline."

"Isn't that what the Fire Chief has said from the beginning?"

"Yes, but now since they know exactly how the fire was set, they are going through their records to see if the method used at Kroner's matches other cases. They say each arsonist tends to have his or her particular, what they call, fingerprint."

"Makes sense, doesn't it?" I said. "Why mess with success? And speaking of success, how are you progressing with identifying the body?"

I could almost see the exasperated look on his face. "No luck so far. And I'm not sure how we are going to proceed. Sheldon Junior did a preliminary autopsy, and then shipped the body over to the state lab. Unfortunately, they're never in a hurry, so who knows when we will get that report. Sheldon said the body was so badly burned, any ID is going to be difficult."

"Can't they check dental records or use DNA testing?" I suggested.

"Like we're going to ask every dentist in the country to go through his records. We will check with Boise, but I have a feeling that was just a stopping-off place for her. And as far as DNA testing, that is an expensive procedure, and I'm not sure where I could get the funds."

"Maybe the lawyers for the estate would chip in," I said. "They surely want to get this cleared up."

"I'm pretty sure that would be a conflict of interest. But you're correct, nothing can be done about settling the estate until we identify the body and find out who did her in."

"Do you think the secondary legatees—you know, Floyd and the minister—had something to do with the fire and murder? That's what some people around town are saying."

"Now, Jessie, it is much too soon to speculate."

"You know what I think?"

"No, I don't, and I'm pretty sure I don't want to."

"Too bad," I said. "I'm going to tell you anyway. I think this extends further than a battle over Fred Kroner's estate. Anyway, if you get your report in time, come on over. I promise not to bug you about the case."

"That'll be the day. Miss you." And with that he hung up.

I put my groceries away, leaving out enough to have a simple stir fry for dinner. The fresh produce at the market was pretty sad, so I was resorting to prepackaged frozen veggies. Maybe tomorrow night Gil would come over, and I could make him some down-home comfort food. He sounded like he needed it.

As I stirred my dinner in the wok, I thought about what I had said to Gil and why I had said it. I knew the conversation at the Library Board meeting had provoked it.

I dished up my stir fry and carried it over to the table. A sliver of moon, etched against the black sky, was the only thing visible out the window. I looked over my shoulder at the computer in the corner. In the morning. *Emily Says* was beckoning.

CHAPTER 11

" 'Emily, Emily, where are you?' Karen yelled. 'I have a terrible problem.' "

I said the words under my breath. I started every *Emily Says* story the same way. Emily's friend Karen would burst into the house claiming dire consequences if Emily did not help her. This time Freddy, a fourth-grader, was trying to intimidate the third-graders at Adams Elementary School.

I leaned back from my computer, trying to imagine what Freddy looked like. He would be short for a fourth-grader, but still tall enough to threaten the younger children. His body was pudgy and soft, the result of too much fast food and sugar-laden snacks. His skin had a gray cast. It had been a long time since he had had a good scrubdown. His permanent front teeth were oversized for his face, and they had come in crooked, giving him the look of a beaver in need of orthodontia. Bits of food were embedded around the gum line. A month earlier he had been sent home with a note saying he had head lice and was not to come back to school until they were eradicated.

The next paragraph was also a near duplicate in each Emily story. Her fans had come to expect it. New readers needed the explanation. Just the same, I read it out loud.

"It was silly of Karen to wonder where Emily was. Everybody knew how to find Emily. If she wasn't at school or eating dinner with her mother and father, she was sitting at the little table in the corner of the family room reading the *Encyclopedia Britan-*

nica. Emily loved being an authority. She vowed to learn everything in the world. Whenever she asked her father a question, he always said, 'Look it up in the encyclopedia,' so now she went straight to the source. She was currently on volume six. She could have gone on the Internet, but there was something satisfying about being able to turn the pages and trace a sentence with her finger."

I reviewed my mental picture of Freddy. Something about it was strangely familiar. The more I thought about it, the more I was convinced that the description came from something out of my past. As I swiveled around in my chair, it hit me. The little boy I had described was the spitting image of Floyd Kroner at age nine.

What was this fixation on Floyd? He was even interfering with my Emily story. I hadn't thought about him in years and now, everywhere I turned, I ran into him or heard about him. He had even invaded my subconscious. Well, he did always have sort of a neglected look about him when he was a kid, but the head lice thing was totally from my imagination.

Thinking about Floyd reminded me of the service Reverend Smythe was holding Sunday evening. Hadn't Allie said she watched him on television? I would rather stay home and watch than go over to the Abundant Life Church. I needed to call her and find out what station it was on. I looked at the clock. It was eight-thirty. Still early enough to call. Nine was the unofficial cutoff for social calls in Riverport.

Booter answered the phone. When I asked for Allie, he said, "She's off in the study reading her Bible. She's been at it since supper. I guess she's afraid the reverend is going to give her a pop quiz when she sees him Sunday."

I gave what I hoped was an appropriate chuckle. "This is Jessie Schroeder. Do you think she'd mind talking to me for a couple of minutes?"

"Hell no, Jessie. Just hang on."

I knew from past calls to the Bowman household to get the phone away from my ear immediately, because Booter started yelling at a volume that would shatter glass or at least an eardrum before he laid the receiver down. "Allie, honey. Phone. Jessie Schroeder needs to talk to you."

I could hear Allie's heels clicking on the wooden floor as she came to the phone. Only Allie would wear high heels at home.

"What are you doing calling me on a Friday night? You should be out on the town with that handsome sheriff of yours."

"Duty comes before pleasure, I'm afraid," I said. "I need some information from you."

"Me?"

Allie sounded amazed that anyone would want information from her.

"You mentioned at the Board meeting that you watch Reverend Smythe on his Sunday shows. What channel is it on?"

"Channel 11 at seven o'clock. I never miss it. 'Course I will this Sunday 'cause I'm going to see him in person. I am so excited. Booter, bless his heart, got some seats right up front. Say, why don't you come with us? We've got one ticket left."

I hesitated for a minute then decided. "Why, I'd love to."

"Oh, goodie. I can promise you, you won't regret it!" she shouted, "Hey, Booter, Jessie's coming with us to see Reverend Smythe. Isn't that fabulous?"

A moment of silence, then Allie returned. "Booter says to tell you we'll pick you up at six-thirty."

"Nonsense, I'm out of your way. I'll meet you there."

"No way. A lady should not be driving around by herself after dark. It's not safe. See you Sunday," Allie said and hung up before I could object again.

Saturday turned out to be a less eventful day than I had hoped for. Gil came over for dinner, and we had no sooner settled down in front of the fireplace to finish our bottle of wine than he yanked off his pager.

"Damn that Clarence. I need to call in."

I waited impatiently for him to return, though I had a feeling it would be to say goodbye instead of settling back on the sofa with me. Unfortunately, I was correct.

"Some big ruckus going on at Smitty's. Those river rats don't have enough to do in cold weather, so they spend their time drinking and beating the shit—sorry about that—out of each other. Clarence says there are some pretty serious knives being flashed around. I should close that place down. But there is an advantage of letting Smitty's stay open. It gives the rats a place to go, so they're not pounding on their wives and kids. Plus he's got the best barbecue in town."

"Why don't I cork the bottle? We can finish it when you come back."

"From the sound of things, I won't be back. Why don't you save it and we can have it tomorrow night?"

"Uh." I stammered for a minute. "I'm not going to be home tomorrow night. The Bowmans, Allie and Booter, asked me to go to some program at the Abundant Life Church with them." I wasn't about to tell him I had essentially initiated the invitation. "Allie is on the Library Board with me and Booter's been really nice to me ever since I came back to Riverport. I couldn't very well say no."

"I find it hard to believe that you are going to spend the evening with the hallelujah crowd." Gil shook his head. "I've got to get going. I'll call."

I walked him to the door, but his lukewarm goodbye kiss showed his mind was already on the way to Smitty's.

I skipped church on Sunday morning. I decided the evening

with Reverend Smythe would more than make up for it. I could count on the fingers of one hand the number of times I went to church in St. Louis, excluding, of course, weddings and that sort of thing. Here I, and most everybody I knew, rarely missed a Sunday. The people of Riverport were no more religious than people elsewhere. It was just that church was an important part of the town's social fiber.

Emily and I had a productive writing session. At the rate I was going, I would be ready for Betsy and Joey next weekend. The story was coming together nicely, especially since I had decided to get rid of Freddy.

Gil called about two to say he still had what seemed like half of the male residents of Bay Road in jail sobering up. He said a couple of their women came in to bail them out, but he convinced them to leave the men with him. "Figured they could use a few more hours of peace. I should be done here by six. Can't talk you out of going to that thing at the Abundant Life, can I?" he asked.

"I'm afraid not, but I'll tell you all about it."

Booter Bowman knocked on the door at exactly 6:30 and escorted me out to his big white Cadillac. The back seat, sheathed in creamy soft leather, was as spacious as a first-class stateroom. The interior light glistened off Allie's fur coat, which I was sure represented the sacrifice of multiple minks. No faux fur for Allie.

"We are thrilled you are coming with us," she said. "It's a good thing Booter got tickets ahead of time, because I am sure there will be a full house."

I mumbled something about how gracious it was of them to include me and settled back for the ten-minute ride.

The parking lot behind the church appeared full, but a man with a flashlight gestured Booter in and led him to a spot right behind the building that was cordoned off with sawhorses.

"Thank you, Everett," Booter said as he got out of the car.

"It's a pleasure, Mr. Bowman," the man said. "You and the ladies just go right in the back entrance there, and the usher'll show you your seats."

The power of money and prestige, I thought, as Booter helped me out of the car. Wonder how much he and Allie give to the Reverend Smythe.

The sanctuary was almost full, but there were three seats, front and center, left for us. To say that all eyes were on us would be an understatement. And wish as I might, it was too late to find a rock to crawl under. To make matters worse, there standing at the corner of the platform, grinning from ear to ear as he watched us, was Floyd Kroner.

I was dying to know who else was there, but my front row seat prevented me from satisfying my curiosity. Instead, I concentrated on the scene in front of me. A simple wooden lectern stood in the center on the semicircular platform, which was engulfed in baskets of flowers and ferns. Poseys by Polley had obviously done a land office business. What looked like giant TVs stood on either side of the platform with the same damn white doves fluttering around the screens that were on the Web site. Allie reached over and squeezed my hand. "Isn't this exciting?" she said.

Before I could answer her, a door in the back of the platform opened and the congregants jumped to their feet and burst into applause and cheers, while I was left sitting and dumbfounded. It was more like a greeting for a rock star or a politician than a minister.

I'd expected Reverend Smythe to be wearing the robes he had had on in the pamphlet I had found, but instead he looked like something out of GQ. His gray pinstripe suit had been carefully tailored and not a wrinkle or crease marred his appearance. It might even be the same suit he was wearing when I saw him in Springfield. His tomato-red tie was held in place by a tie tack that sparkled in the light, and a small enamel American flag was in his left lapel. His cheeks were smooth and rosy, no five o'clock shadow for him, and his salt-and-pepper hair was beautifully groomed, not a piece out of place.

He stood to the side of the podium, arms raised, and waited for the audience to quiet. Only then did he begin. In a voice we all had to strain to hear, he said, "There is room at the cross for every man, woman, and child in this sanctuary." Then the voice increased in volume and repeated the phrase three more times, each time louder than the last.

Everyone's gaze was fastened on Reverend Smythe. Finally, he leaned forward and smiled. "Now that I have everyone's attention," he said, "let's get down to business."

And with that he proceeded to give a surprisingly coherent sermon. There were too many flourishes for my taste and quotes from the scriptures dutifully noted on the screens below the fluttering doves, but all in all it wasn't bad. People carefully wrote down the scripture references and periodically they interrupted him with applause.

After the benediction, he stepped forward and thanked everyone for coming, reminded them of his weekly Sunday show, and suggested they check out the literature and CDs available in the vestibule. No collection had been taken, and all I could surmise was that he made his money off the merchandise.

"Wasn't that wonderful?" Allie said, grasping my arm. "Come on, we get to go meet with him."

Oh, great, I thought. This is probably where the heavy duty money raising is done.

The young man who had shown us to our seats gestured for us to follow him. He took us through a labyrinth of hallways and doors, ending up in a small lounge. Reverend Smythe stood in the center of the room, surrounded by a group of people. A table was set up along the wall bearing a selection of pastries and cookies, a coffee urn, and a punch bowl with a floating ice ring embedded with fruit.

Floyd was at the reverend's side, but he came running over as soon as he saw us. "Jessie, you must meet Reverend Smythe," he said, grabbing my arm and practically dragged me across the room.

Reverend Smythe looked up as we approached and smiled. "Is this the lady we were talking about?" He was a little older than I expected, but quite good looking in a comfortable sort of way.

"Yes, sir. This is my good friend, Jessie Schroeder," Floyd said. "We go way back. All the way to grade school, isn't that right, Jessie?"

I decided to be gracious. "Yes, Floyd and I have known each other a long time," I said and stuck out my hand. "Enjoyed your talk."

"Why, thank you," the reverend said. "And meeting the famous creator of *Emily Says* is a real treat. My niece Caitlin is a huge fan of yours. You have a real gift. Wait till I tell her I met you. Is there a new one in the works?"

"Yes, you can tell Caitlin that a new one should be released on Valentine's Day." I plunged on. "Didn't I see you in Springfield on Tuesday?"

"Tuesday? Oh, yes. One of the board members of God's Fellowship Foundation lives there. I got a call that he had had a heart attack and rushed down to be at his side. Unfortunately, I was too late, but I hope I was able to ease the grieving of the family. Lovely man and much too young."

I waited, expecting him to launch into a litany of "going to a better place" and other such, but he didn't. Instead, he repeated, "Much, much too young.

"And then you had that horrible tragedy here—the fire and the woman who died." He shook his head. "I know the Lord works in mysterious ways, but sometimes I have trouble understanding it. Now, if you will excuse me, I must say hello to the others. And I see my cousin is here."

"See you Wednesday," Floyd said over his shoulder as he followed the reverend across the room to where the Bowmans were talking to Sheldon and Patricia Fowler. Both Patricia and Sheldon's faces lit up in big smiles as he approached. I had never seen Sheldon smile so broadly in all the years I had known him.

Reverend Smythe wrapped his arms around Patricia and give her a big hug and a kiss on the cheek. Isn't that interesting, I thought. Cousins! Kissing cousins at that. The smile had disappeared from Sheldon's face and his shoulders slumped as if he had suddenly assumed the weight of the world. The reverend reached out and patted his arm. The look Sheldon gave him was almost indecipherable. A flash of anger overlaid by a mask of melancholy. What was that all about?

CHAPTER 12

The evening hadn't turned out as I had expected. There was no whooping and hollering, no emotional testimonials, no miraculous cures. Granted it was noisier than Sunday at the Presbyterian Church, but the service had been tightly scripted and produced. Reverend Smythe came across more as a benevolent teacher than a slick marketer.

I watched him make the rounds of the guests at the reception, pausing to talk and listen. I was not so naive that I didn't recognize that he was working the crowd, but his manner was more like that of a college dean visiting with a group of alumni than that of a huckster. All in all I was impressed by his performance. Floyd stayed glued to his elbow, but kept glancing my way. I hoped I had not backed myself into a corner with him.

In the car on the way home, I tried to pry as much information out of Allie and Booter as I could. Keeping Allie on course was not easy.

"I was surprised to find out that Reverend Smythe and Patricia are cousins," I said.

"Isn't that just the most amazing thing? Such an important and amazing man related to someone in our little town. Just amazing. When Patricia mentioned it to me a while back, I was amazed."

I had come to realize that "amazing" was one of Allie's favorite words. It was hard to find anything that she did not find "amazing."

I couldn't resist. "It is amazing," I said. "I know Patricia is from some place in Iowa. Is that where Reverend Smythe grew up?"

"She said they were raised together, closer than fleas on a tick even though he is a bit older than she is, some little town over by Des Moines. She told me the name, but I forgot. Seems his parents were killed in some terrible accident, so her folks took him and his sister in. She said he was always filled with the spirit, even when he was young."

I never did understand what was meant by "filled with the spirit," but decided this was not the time to ask for an explanation.

"It was Reverend Smythe who introduced Patricia and Sheldon. From what I know about Sheldon, he would never have gotten up the nerve to approach her on his own. Laid to rest a lot of rumors around town about him when he got married, if you know what I mean."

I knew what she meant but elected not to comment.

"How did the reverend know Sheldon?" I asked.

"I don't know," Allie said. "I guess the reverend was pretty involved in his church by then, and morticians probably know all sorts of preachers."

"How did Floyd get hooked up with him? From what I remember about Floyd, I find it remarkable that he seems to have gotten religion."

"Now, Jessie, the Lord works in mysterious ways."

Not that mysterious, I thought. *Floyd has to have some ulterior motive, most likely involving money and the inheritance.*

Booter spoke up for the first time. "I got to agree with Jessie. I find it pretty peculiar myself that Floyd has suddenly found religion. Anything that son of a bitch gets interested in tends to come out dirty."

"Now, Booter, I thought we agreed we weren't going to use that kind of language anymore," Allie said.

"Sorry, angel. It's just that that bas . . . , sorry, that fellow raises my hackles. Well, here we are, Jessie. Home the same day!"

He pulled up at the gate and, before I could finish my thank-yous, he was out of the car and holding my door open for me. He took my arm and escorted me up the sidewalk.

"Thanks again, Booter. I'm having lunch with Floyd on Wednesday. If I find out anything interesting, I'll let you know."

"You take care," he said. "And hang on to your valuables. I don't trust that slippery son of a bitch."

I guess Booter figured I didn't have the same sensitivities as Allie.

Genevieve met me with an indignant swish of her tail and stalked over to her empty food bowl. She looked at it, then looked at me, and sat on her haunches expectantly.

I knew better than to make her wait, so before I took off my coat, I poured out her allotment of kibble.

The message light was blinking on the answering machine. I hoped it was Gil, but no such luck. It was Cousin Frank.

"Hey, Cuz. Give me a call. I'll be up till ten."

I looked at my watch. Nine-forty-five. Should I or shouldn't I? Why not? He said ten.

Frank must have been sitting by the telephone because he answered before the first ring had finished.

"Sorry to be calling so late, but I just got home," I said. "What's up?"

"Are you going through the change of life or something, Jessie? First I hear you're having lunch with Floyd Kroner, then I find out you're at the Abundant Life for that God's Fellowship show. What's going on?"

"Gee, I didn't realize I had to clear my social calendar with you."

"I'm going to ignore the sarcasm," Frank said. "You know what I mean."

"I'm not going to ask how you found out about my luncheon. But it wouldn't surprise me if it has been announced on coming community events over WTBA. If you must know, I'm not very happy about spending an hour with Floyd, but it's too late to do anything about it."

"He snookered you, huh?"

"Something like that. Anyway, Booter and Allie asked me to go to the service with them tonight. I hate to say it, but I was pleasantly surprised by the program. It was a pretty calm evening. Reverend Smythe gave a reasonable talk, and he comes across as a nice man. I met him at the reception afterward. Seems his niece is a big fan of *Emily Says*. I had been expecting something like the antics we used to see at the tent revivals we'd sneak into when we were kids. It was a little livelier than the Presbyterians, but not much."

"What's the Bowmans' involvement?"

"Allie is a rabid devotee of the reverend, and you know Booter. Anything Allie wants, Allie gets. I suspect they're major contributors. What I don't understand is why and how Floyd got involved. Maybe I can find out Wednesday."

"What do you mean, how and why Floyd got involved?"

"He's evidently some kind of helper or right-hand man to Reverend Smythe. At least he acts that way."

"Beats me what he's doing," Frank said. "Never known Floyd to participate in any kind of religion. Must be the money thing."

"You're probably right. Do you still want me for dinner on Friday?"

"That's why I called. To remind you. Why don't you come

over about 5:30? Betsy calls every day when she gets home from school to make sure you'll be here."

The next two days were uneventful. Except for my jogs, I stayed close to my computer. Emily and the new storyline had taken over my life. The weather turned nasty, so nasty in fact that I elected to do the three-mile route both days. I promised myself I would make up the miles when the temperature moderated.

Shortly after I got back to the house on Tuesday, a mist started falling. Within the hour, the tree branches were gleaming with a thin coating of ice. The sidewalk leading out to the drive glistened. It looked wet, but I knew better.

I had let the answering machine take most of my calls. There were several from Floyd to remind me of our luncheon date the next day. As if I could forget. I'd given up trying to figure a way out and resigned myself to an hour with Floyd. And, of course, Frank and Aunt Henrietta made their daily check-ins.

Gil called. Clarence was out with the flu, so he was stuck doing double duty. He reported that he was no closer to an identification of the body than he had been a week earlier. A survey of the dentists in Boise and environs had turned up no match on the dental records. The lawyers were bugging him to resolve the mess.

"I don't know what they think I can do," he said. "Wave a magic wand? I've gone online and checked the missing persons reports around the country. Have you any idea how many blond, blue-eyed, five foot five, one-hundred-forty pound women in their thirties are missing in this country? Makes a person wonder if they have a genetic predisposition to disappear."

"It seems to me it makes sense to concentrate on missing reports in the tri-state area. Whoever was at Kroner's place came by automobile. No other way to get there unless they walked."

"Hmmm, good suggestion. Of course, they could have flown in to one of the cities like St. Louis or Chicago or even Des Moines and rented a car. We also have to consider the possibility that no one has reported her missing."

"That's true, but if there is a report, it would be recent, within the last week. By the way, have you heard back from the arson people?" I asked.

"I already told you what they said."

"I know, I know, but weren't they going to see if the pattern, what did they call it, the fingerprint, of the fire at Kroner's matched other arson cases?"

"Jessie, what are you doing?"

"What do you mean? I'm talking to you."

"It appears to me that you're at it again. You're interrogating me."

"Oops. I guess I'm not supposed to do that," I said. "Sorry."

"That's all right. I'd think you were sick if you didn't put me through twenty questions. Listen, I've got to go. It's getting really bad on the streets. Don't go out unless it's absolutely necessary. I don't know what it is about an ice storm that inspires people to jump in their cars and start driving around as fast as they can, but it seems half the population of Spencer County is busy smashing into each other or sliding into ditches. Stay warm. I miss you." With that he hung up.

The tree branches were starting to sag under the weight of the ice. If this kept up, chances were good the power lines would snap. I had some wood beside the fireplace, but decided to get the carrier and bring more into the house. Fortunately, the woodpile was right beside the back door. Genevieve accompanied me to the door, but as soon as she stuck her nose outside, she made a quick pivot and headed back to her warm cushion, complaining all the way.

I stepped out and went skittering across the ice like a water bug on a pond. Only a quick grab of the doorknob saved me from a full-body slalom across the back patio. The woodpile was sheathed in ice. I would need a pick axe to loosen the logs, so I decided to emulate Genevieve and head back indoors. I could make do with my kerosene heater if I lost power. I hated the smell, but the prospect of freezing was an alternative I hated even more. I got out the Coleman lantern out of the pantry, just in case.

I went over to my computer to make sure I had my manuscript backed up. And then, like the man who wore both a belt and suspenders, I printed out a hard copy. I was haunted by the fear that I would never be able to duplicate my words and ideas. I assumed that once out of my mind, they floated into the ether, never to be seen again.

The story was coming together nicely, and I should have a rough draft finished by Friday to tell to the kids. I worked for several more hours before I called it quits, but not before I backed up everything again. It was not quite five o'clock, and already dark. I turned on the radio to WTBA in time to hear Harry Simon's silky baritone announce that Sheriff Gil Keller had declared a state of emergency. The next thing I heard was Gil's voice.

"At four P.M. I declared an official state of emergency for the entire area of Riverport and Spencer County. All private automobile and truck travel is banned until further notice. In case of emergency, dial 911. All emergency vehicles are equipped with chains, and we will reach you. Do not, I repeat, do not try to drive yourself. People with cell phones, please make sure they are fully charged and that you have fresh batteries in your portable radios. All backup systems are in place at police headquarters.

"The roads, streets, and sidewalks are heavily coated in ice. Conditions are extremely dangerous and getting worse. Please stay indoors. We have multiple reports of downed trees and branches and several roads are blocked. If you see a downed power line, call authorities. Do not approach. Please, everybody. Be careful."

Harry Simon came back on. "Stay tuned to WTBA. We will keep you up-to-date as we receive storm and damage information. Now for a little music."

As I turned off the radio, I heard a loud crack and then a thud. I looked out the window in time to see a huge branch settling over the fence amidst a shower of ice crystals. Fortunately, it missed the power and phone lines coming into the house. Heeding Gil's words, I dug my cell phone out of my purse and plugged in the charger. I had used my cell phone so little since I moved back to Riverport that I rarely thought to check the charge. I found a fresh package of AA batteries and put them next to my portable radio.

I went back to the window. The beam from the pole light bounced off the sheet of ice that covered the barnyard. I was grateful I had no animals to take care of like Frank. "Wonder how they're doing," I muttered and went to the phone to call them.

"Hi there, Jessie," Frank said before I could identify myself. I always forgot they had caller ID.

"How are things at your house?"

"Few branches down, but so far not too bad. How about you?"

"Same as you. Did you get your livestock in the barn?"

"Yeah, but I was glad no one was around with a video or I would be a prime candidate for *Funniest Home Videos*. My arms and legs were going every which way. Needed some of those crampon things that mountain climbers use. My advice is stay inside. Gotta go. Wilma's hollering for me."

I'd no sooner hung up than the phone rang.

"Jessie, it's Gil. I just have a minute. Are you okay?"

"So far. Got a big branch down, but nothing else. How are things going?"

"It's a mess. I wanted you to know that you don't need to show up for your lunch date tomorrow. Floyd crashed his Hummer into a telephone pole and he's in pretty bad shape. May not make it."

"Oh my God! What happened?"

"I'm not sure. He was coming down the hill toward Front Street. He evidently went into a skid. Must have been going forty when he hit the pole. And the fool wasn't wearing a seat belt. He needs to be air lifted to Springfield, but Lord knows when we can get a copter in."

CHAPTER 13

I stood staring at the telephone long after Gil said goodbye. Floyd's condition sounded grim. Much as I had hoped for something to cancel our lunch, this was carrying things to extremes.

What in the world had he been doing driving around in this mess? Only a fool would have attempted that hill in an ice storm. Floyd was an ass, but he was no fool. The incline felt almost perpendicular as the street came over the lip of the bluff and on down to the river. It gave me pause even on a bright sunny day. At least once a year, usually on a Saturday night, someone came flying down right into the bay. Fortunately, the water was shallow at that point.

It had turned dark. The snap and pings of the ice-shrouded twigs bouncing off the metal roof sounded like I had a timpanist practicing overhead. I went to the pantry and moved the Coleman lantern to the kitchen counter. I had put on the propane cylinder earlier and checked the mantle. It was ready to go. And my flashlight, with fresh batteries, and a packet of matches for the stove and heater were in my pocket. In the good old days my method of preparation would have been to sit with my fingers crossed, hoping the storm would pass me by.

Not for the first time I thought about how my life had changed. That was not quite correct. I was the one who had changed. I no longer waited for events to sweep me along. I was the one who wielded the broom. I found myself smiling.

Jeez, Jessie, aren't you the pontificator? I thought. Keep going like this and you can audition for an advice columnist, dishing out "take control of your life" and things like that to the confused and lovelorn.

Well, it's true, I came back, I have changed.

Before I could debate further with myself, the lights flickered several times and then gave up the ghost, leaving me in darkness. I lit the lantern and moved it over to the kitchen table by the window. The draft around the old wooden window frame provided enough fresh air so I didn't risk asphyxiation.

I stared out into the black void. The question is there such a thing as a white void crossed my mind? Or blue? Or red? What to do? Genevieve had settled into my lap. She would be perfectly happy if I did nothing but gently scratch her neck. I found myself thinking about Floyd and the whole Kroner mess. Might as well. I couldn't do much else until the power came back on.

Was the body really Johanna Kroner? I didn't understand enough about medical forensics to know how the experts would go about proving or disproving her identity. Surely, with all the new knowledge about DNA, there must be some way to take samples from the uncles or Floyd and compare them with the body's. I knew it was possible to trace a relationship down the male line of a family, but something I had read made me think it was more difficult to trace from male to female.

I wondered how Fred Kroner had found out about the long-lost niece. Had she gotten in touch with him or had he hired a search service? But why would he spend money on a search, if he didn't have reason to believe she existed? Someone must have suggested it to him, but who? And how do you find out if someone actually exists? Hire a private investigator? Maybe the genealogists had procedures to follow? There was nothing in the boxes I had gone through so far that suggested any leads. My head was filled with more questions than answers, and no way to get in touch with someone who could help me. I made a mental note to call Patricia Fowler when the weather settled down. She had the reputation of being the genealogy guru of Riverport. In fact, I wondered if Patricia had something to do with it.

Then there was the Reverend Smythe and Floyd. Where did they fit into the picture? If there was no Johanna or she was dead, they stood to inherit a large chunk of money. But what if Floyd died? Who inherited? His father and uncle? Or would it all go to the reverend and God's Fellowship? My head was beginning to ache.

Genevieve stretched and circled my lap, more concerned with her comfort than mine. "Of course she is," I muttered. "She's a cat." I moved her to another chair and went to the sink to fill the kettle with water. The advantage of a gas stove was I could light the burners with a match even with the electricity out. A cup of tea was what I needed. I rarely drank tea, but tonight it felt like a good idea. Something about a storm called for tea, not coffee.

I rummaged through the cabinet and found a box of tea bags. Lord knew how long they had been there. I let a bag soak in the boiling water until the color looked suitably muddy, added a dab of honey, and carried the cup over to the table.

No sooner had I lifted the cup to my lips than someone or something started pounding on my door. I let out a yelp and sloshed hot liquid down my front and onto the table.

"Who's there?" I yelled as I went over to the door, pulling my sweater away from my chest to ease the burning.

"Please let me in," a male voice said. I decided this was no time for timidity and yanked open the door.

To say I was speechless is an understatement as a muddied and bloodied Reverend Smythe stumbled into my kitchen.

"Oh, thank God," he said as he bumped into the table and

collapsed into a chair, spilling the rest of the tea. "Yours is a beacon of hope shining in the wilderness."

"What are you doing here?" I finally blurted. "I thought you left yesterday."

A closer look at him convinced me that further questions could wait. He was obviously in distress. His trousers were shredded at the knees and stained with blood from his scraped knees, and his hands were bleeding. I ran into the living room and grabbed an afghan off the couch to wrap around him. His jacket was more suited to a spring evening than a wretched Midwestern ice storm and his leather shoes belonged behind a pulpit, not breaking a trail through ice. I quickly made another cup of tea and held it to his lips. His hands were shaking too hard to steady it. I lit the kerosene heater and moved it over close to him.

"What happened?" I asked as his shaking eased.

He shook his head and held out the cup for a refill. "You'd think an Iowa boy would know better," he said. "Guess I've been in the city too long."

I made more tea, a pot this time, and poured us each a cup.

"I was almost back to Springfield when Patricia called me on my mobile and told me Floyd had been in a terrible accident. I had stayed over an extra day to visit with her and Sheldon. When I left Riverport, the ice storm was just starting. I figured I could outdrive it, and I had. Anyway, when I heard about Floyd, I knew my place was at his side so I turned back. He's a strange little man, but he has heard God's call."

I decided not to interrupt yet. He needed to get his story out.

"The ice got worse the closer I came to Riverport, but I've got an SUV with four-wheel drive, so I was doing okay. Then a couple of miles out of town, a big tree was down, blocking the highway. I'd just passed a blacktop, and I figured it would take me into town the back way. Big mistake. I hadn't been on it a mile when I went into a skid and ended up in the ditch."

"Why didn't you stay with your car?" I asked.

"Well, the SUV was on its side, and I was almost out of gas. Another big mistake. I should've filled up before I turned back. Like I said, I've been a city boy too long. I managed to crawl out a window and back up to the road. I saw a glimmer of light. Thought it was a mirage at first, but then something told me that the good Lord was looking out for me. Took me a long time, but His hand guided me to your door."

"You're a lucky man," I said, "but we've got to get you out of those wet clothes and into a hot shower."

The look on his face at my suggestion was one of shock. It never occurred to me that a man of the cloth might take offense at my suggestion. In fact, it didn't matter to me one way or another. I didn't want him succumbing to hypothermia in my kitchen.

"You're about the same size as my dad was. Some of his things are still here." Actually, many of his clothes were still in the big cedar closet upstairs. Mom could never bear to get rid of them.

I didn't wait for his assent and escorted him up the stairs and into the bathroom. I put a candle lantern on the back of the commode.

"I'll leave the clothes right outside the door, and while you are showering, I'll call the Sheriff. He needs to know about the accident. I'll tell him where the car is and that you're all right. Don't worry about using up the hot water. I have a gas heater, so take your time." I was tempted to say, I promise not to peek, but didn't.

I got a wool shirt and corduroy pants out of the closet along with a t-shirt, wool socks and slippers. He would have to do without underwear. I left them outside the bathroom and went back downstairs to call Gil.

My cell phone was fully charged, and I called the nonemergency number. I was amazed when Virginia answered the phone as calmly and matter-of-factly as if it were a normal day.

"Spencer County Sheriff's Office. How may I direct your call?"

"Virginia, this is Jessie Schroeder. How on earth did you get to the office?"

"Hi there, Jessie. My husband Norman fixed up some chains for my bicycle and I just rode right over. It's only a couple of blocks. They worked so well, I called him and told him he should apply for one of those patents. How're you doing out there in the country?"

"I'm fine. The power and phone line are gone. I'm pretty well fixed, but I need to report an accident. No injuries, but the Reverend Smythe slid off the road into a ditch close to my place. He saw the lantern in my window and made it here. I wanted the Sheriff to know that if anyone reported the car, he didn't need to worry about it."

"What in the world was he doing out your way?"

"He'd heard about Floyd's accident and was trying to get back into Riverport to be at his side. Oh, and tell the Sheriff that there is a tree blocking the highway just east of the blacktop that comes past my place. That's why the reverend ended up here."

"Will do. That reverend's lucky he's not sharing a hospital room with Floyd. You want the Sheriff to call you?"

"No, that's okay. I'm going to turn off my cell to preserve the battery. I'll call if there is a problem. Let's hope for a warm, sunny day tomorrow to melt off this mess."

"Amen to that, Jessie. Take care."

The aroma of moth balls preceded Reverend Smythe into the kitchen. My mom had made sure that any moth that made it into the cedar closet would never survive.

"Feeling better?" I asked. I must have misjudged his height, because the cuffs of Dad's pants were dragging on the floor. Then I noticed that he was shorter than I. When we had met at the reception we had seen eye to eye. Ah, I thought, he had been wearing lifts.

"Much," he said. "I can't thank you enough for taking me in. You are a true Christian."

"What I did had nothing to do with religion, Reverend. It was the humane thing to do." What possessed me to make such a statement, I don't know.

He looked at me for a moment. "*Touché*, Miss Schroeder. Point well taken. Now, do you think I could have another cup of that tea?"

"Sorry about that," I said. "I didn't mean to sound combative. Is there someone you need to call? Someone who was expecting you? Your wife?"

"That is kind of you to offer, but no one is expecting me. And, alas, I have yet to find a woman who can put up with me."

"I'll fix a fresh pot," I said. "I'm going to fortify mine with some bourbon. It's going to be a long, cold night. How about you?"

"Sounds good."

I was surprised. I had expected him to say "no thank you" and something about setting an example for his congregants.

I poured us each a generous dollop and carried the mugs over to the table. The kerosene heater was putting out a pathetic little circle of heat. Not for the first time, I wished the old wood stove that used to stand in the corner was still there. I made a promise to myself that I was going to reinstall one in the kitchen. I was happy to have Genevieve curl up in my lap.

"Allie Bowman tells me you and Patricia are cousins," I said. "That you grew up together."

"We're actually not cousins, but when I was fourteen and my

sister ten, our mom and dad were killed in an auto accident, and Patricia's parents took us in. My father was pastor of the Methodist church in Walnut Creek where they lived. Sis and I had no other family that we knew of. Even Patricia with her passion for genealogy has been unable to find any living relatives out there. Every line seems to have died out."

"When did you meet Sheldon? Allie Bowman tells me you played matchmaker with him and Patricia."

He laughed. "I just introduced them and let nature take its course. I've known Sheldon since he was in college. We met when he signed up for a retreat I was running. Good man. He serves on the board of God's Fellowship Foundation. Patricia's lucky."

I looked at my watch. It was after ten. "I need to check my phone for messages, then I think we'd better turn in. I have plenty of goose down comforters, so we should be all right."

As I suspected, there was a message from Gil—cryptic as usual. "Call me."

I dialed the number of his mobile phone and he answered immediately.

"Virginia gave me your message. Is everything all right?"

"Reverend Smythe was lucky. He went into the ditch just beyond the house, where the road starts uphill to Frank's place. He saw my light and made it here, pretty cold but otherwise fine. He was trying to get back to Riverport to be with Floyd."

"Tell him that they've got Floyd stabilized, and the copter is supposed to come first thing in the morning to transfer him to Springfield. It's going to be a long night, but at least people are staying off the roads. They've opened the gym at the high school and brought in cots and blankets for anyone who's stranded. Don't know when the power will be back, but the crews are out now."

"Sounds like you have things under control," I said.

"Yeah, but I sure wish I was with you. Never thought I'd be jealous of an evangelical minister. You make sure he behaves himself."

"Honestly, Gil, what a thing to say."

"Can't help it. Somehow, I'll be out first thing in the morning. Miss you."

"Me, too," I said, wishing I could say more, but Reverend Smythe was hovering at my elbow.

CHAPTER 14

I awoke with a start. A smoke alarm was shrieking downstairs, there was a terrible stench in the air, and I could hear a man yelling my name.

I sat bolt upright and fought my way out of the mound of covers heaped on the bed. I grabbed my robe and stuffed my feet into slippers. A belch of smoke came through the door when I opened it. I slid and ran down the staircase and came face to face with Reverend Smythe standing at the foot looking distressed. The front door was wide open.

"I made a stupid mistake," he said.

"What happened?"

"I thought a fire in the fireplace would take the chill off the place, but I guess I forgot to open the flue and then I couldn't find it, so I threw some water on the fire, and then, well, you can see for yourself."

I picked my way through the smoke into the living room and twisted and pushed the handle on the face of the fireplace. In an instant the smoke reversed and started going up the chimney.

"Go open the kitchen doors, and I'll get a window in the dining room."

The reverend started to say something, but I'm sure the expression on my face made him think better of it. Instead he turned and dashed to the kitchen.

What a mess! The smoke was thinning, but I knew I would have a woodsy smell for quite some time. Fortunately, it didn't look bad enough that I would have to call in the experts. The smoke alarm finally quit whining.

I stepped out on the front porch. The sun was coming over the trees. Every branch, twig, and blade of grass glistened, and beams of light bounced around the yard like reflections off a fine-cut diamond. How could something so beautiful be so destructive? The scene was splendid; it was hard to be angry, even at an idiot who didn't know to open the fireplace flue before he lit a fire. I walked back in the house. The reverend was standing in the front hall. The look on his face reminded me of a puppy who had done something bad on the rug and was waiting to be whipped.

"It's not so bad, Reverend. Let's fix us some coffee."

I filled the pot with water and hauled out the mortar and pestle out of the cupboard. We would have to pulverize the beans by hand, since I only had whole beans. "Here, you take care of this," I said, pouring the beans into the mortar. "We'll have to rough it till the power comes back on."

"Please forgive me," he said. "I'll pay for any restoration you need. And do you think you could call me John. Every time you refer to me as *Reverend* Smythe, I feel like I should lead us in prayer."

I had to laugh at that. "John it is. I don't think the smoke is going to be a problem. Let's close up the house now. What I need is coffee. After I get caffeinated, we can get that wet wood out of the fireplace and have a real fire. No telling how long until the power is back."

He went to work on the coffee beans with a vengeance. No doubt he was trying to prove he was good for something. That was fine with me. Getting the coffee brewed ranked at the top of life's necessities for me.

While John (I was having trouble converting my form of address from Reverend to John) continued to pulverize the coffee beans, I checked my messages on my cell phone. There was a new one from Gil.

"Sorry, Hon, I can't come by till later. There's been a bad accident out on the Interstate. No serious injuries, but cars and trucks are strewn every which way. I don't know when we will get it sorted out. If preacher boy is still there, and I assume he is, tell him to call Cal's Towing. They'll get his car out, and he can be on his way. Floyd's on the copter to Springfield, so he can catch up with him there."

I reported Gil's information to John, modifying some of the language and wondering as I did at the sarcasm of his words. If I didn't know better, I'd think Gil was jealous.

"Let's have that coffee before we go any further," I said. "And then I'll fix us some breakfast. Can't have you facing the world on an empty stomach. Oh, and when you call Cal, tell him to pick you up here. No sense making that icy trek again."

I was hoping while we ate breakfast that I could get him talking about the Kroner estate and how his group had gotten involved.

"Let me cook breakfast," John said. "I'm pretty handy with a skillet. How about a nice cheese omelet with bacon and toast, if you have the makings?"

"You're on."

Opening the refrigerator was no problem. First, as usual, there was little food so spoilage was not a danger, and, second, it was about as cold outside the box as it was in.

He scrounged through the vegetable crispers and extracted several limp scallions, half a green pepper that was in the process of self-destructing, and a handful of wrinkled mushrooms. He also found a slightly desiccated chunk of cheddar cheese.

"Ah, these will do nicely," he said.

I watched him deftly trim and chop like a professional chef while the bacon sizzled in the skillet. He whipped the eggs with a fork. I had to confess that I did not own a whisk.

"Why don't you make the toast while I finish this up," he said.

"I'm afraid I can't. No electricity, remember?"

He nodded. "How soon we forget. Butter a couple slices of bread and I will fry them up."

"That I can do. How many?"

In a few minutes, I was presented with a perfect omelet, speckled with chopped vegetables and oozing cheese, crispy bacon, and the fried bread.

"Eat up," he said, "before it gets cold."

I needed no further encouragement.

"That was wonderful," I said as I shined the plate with my last bit of toast. "Where did you learn to cook so well?"

"Working my way through college, I had a night job as a counter cook in a diner. Taught me a lot about cooking and human nature."

"I guess in your business it pays to know how to interpret human nature." As soon as the words were out of my mouth, I realized how crass that sounded. Well, it probably did pay.

"I mean, it must be a real asset."

"That it is. That it is," he said. "Counter cooks in all-night diners and bartenders probably have a better grasp of human nature than most psychologists."

I didn't quite know how to move the conversation in the direction I wanted. After considering several different subtle entrees, I decided to be my usual blunt self.

"I'm curious. Your organization, God's Fellowship, how do people find out about it? I know you have a Web site, but what else do you do to spread the word? Does your membership and support come mostly from your television and radio programs or is your resident congregation responsible?"

He looked at me and paused as if weighing his words before

he answered. "Oh, we have an active outreach program," he finally said.

I didn't respond right away. In my former life in St. Louis, before I escaped into children's literature, I had been an officer in a public relations company. I was well aware that active outreach could take many forms from subtle suggestion and half truths to power arm twisting and threats and everything in between.

"Active outreach takes a lot of time and energy," I said.

"That it does," he said.

I decided to take my queries a step further. "How did Fred Kroner get involved in God's Fellowship? Everyone around here is amazed that he included you in his will. Fred was not known for his altruism. That's quite a pile of money you will get, if the body actually turns out to be this long-lost niece Johanna Kroner."

He gave me a look I couldn't fathom. The jolly fellow well-met persona was slipping away. He finally smiled thinly and said, "I gave up a long time ago trying to figure out what makes people open their pocketbooks. Why one person will be generous to a fault while another is the exact opposite, but then again I never met Mr. Kroner. If anyone could tell you what motivated him, it would be Patricia. She is our number-one booster and recruiter."

"Patricia?"

"She's the outreach coordinator for Spencer County and an enthusiastic follower of Colossians 3:23."

"I'm afraid I don't know what that is," I said.

"It says 'Whatever your task, work heartily, as serving the Lord and not men.' And believe me, she takes the 'work heartily' seriously. She's always on the lookout for lonely souls to rescue. I guess her experience in the mortuary business has made her aware of the poor souls who have no one to grieve for them when they leave this world, so she brings them membership in our family."

I didn't quite know how to reply to that. Did entry into the "family" require a promise of money now and in the future? I was reminded of pleas from my alma mater and various not-for-profits. Make a legacy gift, they suggested. We will handle all of the paperwork. Did Patricia walk around with the forms in her purse? Was she disappointed when God's Fellowship was relegated to second place, after Johanna Kroner? Did she work heartily to make sure the obstacles to the Fellowship receiving the millions were cleared out of the way? Oh, my God, Jessie. Don't be absurd.

"That surprises me," I said. "She seems a quiet person. Actually, I don't know her too well. Sheldon Junior is on the Library Board with me. Which reminds me, I've been meaning to ask you. Was Sheldon with you at the hotel in Springfield, you know, the night Fred Kroner's house burned down? I was sure I saw him in the parking lot."

"Really?" he said and abruptly changed the subject. "Now, may I use your cell phone to call this Cal? I'd better be on my way. If it's all right, I'll wear these clothes home you've loaned me, then mail them back."

I quickly determined if I continued to push the issue of the hotel in Springfield, it would get me nowhere. "Don't bother. I'm sure you have an alms box they can go into."

He looked at me blankly for a minute before he said, "Of course."

I was tempted to ask, "You do have an alms box, don't you? Or doesn't God's Fellowship's active outreach include the poor and needy?" but instead turned on the cell phone and handed it to him along with the phone book. I was beginning to decide I didn't like Reverend Smythe as much as I thought, even though he made a mean omelet.

Arrangements were made for the tow. I was amazed at how quick Cal said he would arrive. Made me wonder if Gil had told him to put the preacher at the top of the list. The sun was doing its job, and the ice was rapidly softening. Every few minutes there was a shower of ice as a branch unburdened itself and snapped back into position. I had a lot of debris in the yard, but it didn't look like I had lost anything significant except that one big limb.

Reverend Smythe (I had reverted to referring to him by his title) had gone upstairs to get his things. I heard him coming back as Cal pulled into my lane, the ice crust cracking beneath the weight of his truck.

"Let me get you a bag to put those things in," I said as he entered the kitchen with his bundle of clothes. I was correct about the lifts in his shoes because now we were seeing eye to eye to each other again.

"You have been incredibly kind. Thank you," he said as he held out his hand.

"No problem. If you get tired of spreading the Word, you can always get a job as a cook. I'll vouch for you." A dumb thing to say, but he smiled and made his way gingerly down the walk to Cal's tow truck.

I'm sure there was no relationship, but as the truck went down the lane, the electricity came back on. The refrigerator started humming and the furnace fan whirred back into action. Genevieve stuck her nose out of her kitty house as if she knew it was safe to come back out. I poured myself a cup of coffee, reheated it in the microwave, and carried it over to the table. What a curious night and morning.

I was disappointed with myself when I thought back on my attempted interrogation of the reverend. Maybe it was the cold that had made me so heavy handed. I certainly had not found out anything significant, though it was interesting how he had clammed up when I tried to get information about God's Fellowship and the relationship with Fred Kroner and especially when I asked him about Sheldon. The reference to Patricia was interesting. I wondered if I could get her to talk to me.

CHAPTER 15

The ice was melting, but it was still dangerous to venture outdoors. I also decided to wait to turn on my computer. I wanted to make sure the power wasn't going off again. Now that the furnace was running, I reopened the front door. The smoky haze had pretty well cleared, but it smelled like I was sitting around a camp fire. There were streaks of soot on the front of the fireplace and ashes on the apron, but that would be easy to clean.

Reverend Smythe had managed to get out of the house without helping unload the wet wood. That was all right. I had been ready for him to leave. The wood would dry. I tried the regular phone line, but it was still dead.

Genevieve was following me around, meowing. It could only mean one thing—"feed me." I spooned out her morning treat of half a can of wet food, and then went upstairs to prepare for the day. It was still freezing in my bedroom, so I didn't take long to get my clothes on, including a heavy fleece shirt that was usually too warm to wear indoors. I'd wait to shower until the house temperature returned to normal. That reminded me to check the bath and bedroom that the reverend had used.

He had stripped the bed and neatly folded and stacked the comforters. He had also folded the used towels and carefully wiped down all the bathroom fixtures. Someone had taught him well. There was nary a fingerprint or smudge to be seen on the chrome. The phrase "nary a fingerprint or smudge" repeated itself in my head. The plastic change holder in the purse found at the fire! Had it been checked for fingerprints? Surely all the contents had been tested. Did I dare ask Gil?

I went back into the bedroom to get the sheets. Might as well run them through the washer while I was thinking about it. When I bent over and scooped up the pile of sheets and pillowcases, something fell out, hit my foot, and slid under the bed. I knelt on the throw rug and peered under the bed, but it was so dark, all I could see were dust bunnies. "Damn," I muttered and went to get the flashlight.

Back on my hands and knees, I shined the light under the bed. At first I could see nothing, but gradually made out a dark lump close to the wall. The dark-stained oak floors made perfect camouflage. I flattened myself and squirmed under the bed, accumulating the dust bunnies on my fleece shirt on my way in.

Scuttling back out, I sat cross-legged on the rug and looked at a small, hand-tooled leather address book. Embossed on the front cover in gold were the initials JWS. John W. Smythe. I turned it over in my hands. I would have to get in touch with him and tell him I had it. Probably the easiest route would be to call Patricia and let her orchestrate the return. It would also give me the perfect excuse to talk to her.

I started to slip the book into my pocket, but stopped. I wondered whose names a minister would keep in his personal address book. Now, now Jessie, I admonished myself. This is private property. Well, so what. I did find it in my house. Surely, it wouldn't hurt to take a glance. Might be instructive. Besides, I assured myself, I could find the information as to how to return it to the owner.

I sat down on the edge of the bed and turned to the A section. Nothing of interest. The Bowmans were listed under B. There was an asterisk by their name. I kept flipping through the book. Several other names had asterisks. Under the Fs, the

Fowlers were listed, no surprise there, and there was a cell number for Sheldon.

Then the K listing. Floyd Kroner was there. No asterisk. Then Fred Kroner, asterisk. I looked up from the book. Fred Kroner. Hmmm! I thought he said he didn't know the old man. On through the alphabet. Each name was neatly printed in ink, most with a telephone number, but no mailing address, only a zip code.

I made it to the S section. What I saw there, third entry from the top, gave me pause. My name, Jessie Schroeder, with my telephone number and zip code. No asterisk. Why was I in the Reverend Smythe's address book? We had only met two days earlier, and that was in a large social setting.

This was kind of spooky. A man I didn't know had sought refuge in my house, and I gave him shelter and food, not to mention a generous shot of bourbon. But this man I didn't know had my name in his address book. Was this whole episode a setup? *Come on, Jessie, get serious. No one drives his car into a ditch and crawls through an ice storm on purpose. There were many easier ways to get my attention.*

I couldn't just come straight out and ask him why I was included. I would have to admit I looked through the book. Even though I thought it would be a perfect opening to use the found address book as an excuse talk to Patricia, I decided I wasn't going to reveal that I had it, at least not yet.

Let him come looking for it, I thought and slid it back under the bed.

As I came down the stairs, an incredible racket erupted outside. I knew without even looking what was going on. Frank was attacking the downed branches with his chain saw. I threw on my jacket and went outdoors to join him. As soon as he saw me he turned the saw off.

"You got off pretty light," he said. "You want to keep any of this wood?"

"What do you think? You're the expert."

"It's mostly soft maple," he said. "Pretty worthless in the fireplace. I'll haul it off and throw it in the ditch."

The ditch was a bone of contention between me and my cousin. There was a ditch in the pasture that adjoined our two properties. As on many farms, the ditch was the final resting place of the detritus of modern living. I had thrown a fit when I moved back and found old appliances, tin cans, sodden cardboard boxes, and other things I didn't want to examine too closely piled in the ditch.

"This is unacceptable," I had raged. "We're not living in a third world country, though this looks like it. No, wait. I take that back. In a third world country, anything valuable would have been scavenged. Here it just sits and rusts." Frank's argument that the piles of junk halted the erosion in the ditch hadn't convinced me.

We went back and forth and finally reached a compromise. Anything that would biodegrade in good time could go in the ditch while the rest had to be hauled to the landfill. Tree branches qualified for the ditch. That agreement would have to do until Riverport developed a recycling program.

"So, I hear you had a visitor last night," Frank said.

"How in the world did you find out about that?" It never ceased to amaze me how indiscriminately and rapidly news traveled in Spencer County.

"Clarence called me after you spoke with Virginia. He didn't want me to be concerned if I saw the SUV in the ditch. Why didn't you call me? My cell phone was on."

"Well, now just what would you have done?"

"I could have come over. You know, you might have needed help."

"You could have come over! Through a massive ice storm,

over roads that were treacherously slick. Why? To protect your little cousin from being ravaged by a lascivious minister who was so battered and bruised he could barely stand up. Come on, Frank. I've had it with you and Aunt Henrietta assuming that any man who comes through my door is headed straight into my bed."

"Dammit, Jessie, that's not fair. You can sleep with a whole National Guard unit as far as I am concerned. I was thinking about your safety. I could have come across the field in the tractor and brought you both back to my place."

He was correct, of course. He had one of those monster tractors with an enclosed cab—air conditioned in the summer and heated in the winter. It would have been a piece of cake to get to my house.

"Sorry, Frank. I guess I'm being touchy. I should have called, but we were okay."

"Yeah, the problem is I worry about you."

"I know," I said. "I did find out something interesting. It was evidently Patricia Fowler who got old Mr. Kroner interested in God's Fellowship. She and the reverend go back a long way. Her parents raised him and his sister after their parents were killed in an auto accident, and he's the one who introduced her and Sheldon. He said Patricia is one of their biggest recruiters."

"Is that a fact?" Frank said. "Doesn't surprise me a bit. I should have figured that she had something to do with old Mr. Kroner putting God's Fellowship in his will."

"Why do you say that?"

"Well, you know my Mildred, how she accepts everyone and the word 'no' isn't in her vocabulary?"

I certainly did. Every charity and service organization in town had Mildred's name at the top of their list. You needed someone to canvass or solicit or provide refreshments for a fund-raising affair? A phone call to Mildred Schroeder took care of you. You required a sympathetic ear or a helping hand? Mildred was there before you could ask. She was totally non-judgmental. No matter how bizarre your situation, her eyes would get shiny with tears, and with a quick squeeze of her hand she would murmur, "You poor dear, what can I do?"

"One day Mildred ran into Patricia at the market and they got to talking," Frank said. "Mildred came home all bubbly about the exciting work Patricia was doing and before I knew it, Patricia had practically moved in with us."

"What was she doing, trying to recruit Mildred into God's Fellowship?"

"No, not at first. It was that damned genealogy stuff."

"Was this the end of the summer?"

"Yes, that's when it started. Why?" Frank asked.

"Mildred asked to borrow the old Schroeder family Bible." My dad had been the keeper of the family records. When I was little he used to take me through the inked entries that went back to when our ancestors had arrived in this country in the 1840s and tell me family stories. There are a few minor gaps, but nothing significant.

"For about a month that was all Mildred talked about," Frank continued. "Every mealtime was a recitation of what cemetery she had visited or article she had unearthed in the archives of the *Spencer County Argus*. I began to wish I was an orphan with no family.

"Then she abruptly stopped talking about genealogy. Patricia still came by about every day and, let me tell you, I was getting sick and tired of her. Have you ever noticed how she simpers instead of laughing? God, that woman can be irritating."

"What happened?"

Frank didn't answer me right away. He fiddled with the starter on the chain saw. For a minute I thought he was going to ignore my question and start cutting up branches again.

"You know," he said. "There are good people and not so good people and then downright bad people. Well, my Mildred is one of the good people. And sometimes the not so good people and the really bad people try to take advantage of her. Since she would never do such a thing, she doesn't know how to handle it when it happens to her. Am I making any sense?"

I nodded and he continued.

"One night she told me that Patricia had said it was her duty to become a member of God's Fellowship. That she would earn God's grace and life everlasting for only a $500 contribution. She asked me if I thought it was a good idea."

"Let's see if I can guess what you said."

Frank gave me one of his looks that indicated he was going to ignore my comment.

"I'm getting cold. Why don't we go inside," I said. "I'll fix you a cup of coffee and you can tell me about it."

Frank didn't need much encouragement and within minutes he was seated at my kitchen table.

"I don't know, Jessie, I probably overreacted," Frank said after he stirred in the cream and sugar into his coffee. "I'm sure Patricia believes in what she is doing, and I am also sure that Mildred did not discourage her, like you or I would have done. Anyway, I told Mildred absolutely no money was going to that pseudo-religion, we already give plenty to the Presbyterians. The next time Patricia showed up, I told her she was no longer welcome in our house."

I thought for a moment before I answered. "I wouldn't worry about it, Frank. Some people get so wrapped up in their proselytizing that the only way to show them they have overstepped the bounds of propriety is to hit them upside the head with a two by four."

"Yeah, I know, but this is a small town and the Fowlers have been fixtures in the community for a long time. Do you think I should apologize to Patricia?"

"My advice is let sleeping dogs lie. I'm sure Patricia has moved on to another potential convert by now."

"I guess you're right. So tell me, what is this Reverend Smythe like? Pretty amazing that he showed up at your door."

"Well, he's not as slick as I had expected. Pretty nice guy, at least on the surface."

"What do you mean, 'on the surface'?"

"Just that. He holds his cards pretty close to his vest." God, listen to me. Sleeping dogs, close to the vest—I sounded more like Aunt Henrietta all the time.

I started to tell Frank about the address book but decided to discuss it with Gil first, that is if I ever saw him again. It had been days since we had been together.

As if he could read my mind, Frank asked, "So's how the boyfriend? Guess he's been pretty busy with the storm."

"I talked to him earlier this morning. There was a bad accident on the Interstate, cars and trucks everywhere. At least, there weren't any serious injuries. You heard about Floyd?" I asked.

"Clarence told me when he called about Reverend Smythe's SUV last night. Said Floyd was in really bad shape, might not make it. What the hell was he doing driving down that hill during the ice storm and with no seat belt on? Sure beats me."

"Beats me, too," I said.

CHAPTER 16

Frank had almost finished loading the branches when Gil pulled into the lane. I watched as the men exchanged handshakes. Frank leaned forward and said something, then cuffed Gil in the shoulder with his fist. Gil laughed and gave a salute before heading up the walk. He was still grinning when I opened the door.

"What was that about?" I asked.

"Just guy talk. You know Frank."

Unfortunately, I did know Frank, and I was pretty sure he had made a crack about my preacher visitor. "So, are you exhausted?"

"Let's just say I earned my paycheck this past week. First the fire and now the ice storm."

"What do you hear about Floyd?"

"He did arrive in Springfield, but he's still in a coma. It's going to be awhile before they have any kind of a prognosis. The last I heard he was going into surgery. He went right over the airbag and hit the windshield head first."

"Any idea why he was driving around in an ice storm?"

"No, and if he doesn't make it, we never will. Funny thing, though, there were no skid marks at the scene. Just bam, right into the telephone pole."

"Maybe it happened so fast, he couldn't react in time, or he knew it wouldn't help on the ice," I said.

"Maybe, but the automatic response is almost always to slam

on the brakes."

It wasn't like Gil to speculate. For him to express doubt meant he suspected that something was not quite kosher. And there was more.

"Also, I've never known Floyd to drink, except for an occasional beer. The EMS crew who pried him out of the Hummer said he reeked of booze, and there was an empty Jim Beam pint on the floor. None of it makes sense."

I looked at Gil. "Are you suggesting that Floyd was set up?"

"I'm not suggesting anything. It just doesn't make sense."

"I wouldn't be so sure about that. How about this scenario? If both Johanna Kroner and Floyd are out of the way, who gets the whole inheritance? The good reverend, that's who."

The look Gil gave me defied description, but before he could say anything, I held up my hand. "Just speculation. Honest."

Gil shook his head. "I'm too tired to argue today. I assume your preacher made it off okay. Did he give you any trouble?"

I decided to ignore Gil's reference to "my" preacher. "Other than trying to turn the place into a smoke house, no, no problems."

"I thought it smelled a little woodsy. Let me guess. He forgot to open the flue."

"Bingo. All I can say is I hope he uses more common sense in his spiritual counseling."

"Yeah, I hope so too." Gil glanced over my shoulder and frowned. "You know, the whole town is talking about the preacher spending the night here."

"God almighty, Gil. What was I supposed to do? Let him freeze to death? Make him sleep in the barn? He'd been in an accident. He was bruised and bleeding."

"You could have called Frank."

"I could have done a lot of things, but I chose to play Good Samaritan and give him shelter from the cold." I stopped, smiled, and put my arms around him. "If I didn't know better, Gil Keller, I'd say you were jealous."

All I got in response was a grunt and a hug. That was all right. I was happy just to be held.

Finally, Gil spoke. "I've made arrangements for the State Police to cover this weekend. Clarence can handle all the routine matters, and call them in case of emergencies. I'll be off from six P.M. Friday until six P.M. Sunday. I was hoping I could interest you in a weekend activity."

My stomach did a little flip, and I leaned back to look up at him. "The whole weekend?"

"That's what I had in mind. A buddy of mine has a place on the river a little above Nauvoo. Beautiful spot. Nice cabin. Winterized. Fireplace. Private. Interested?"

I couldn't find the right words, so I settled for a nod. Finally, we would have time alone. Really alone. Then I remembered. "Small problem. I agreed to have supper at Frank's Friday, and I can't get out of it. Betsy and Joey will be there and I promised to tell them my new story. I can't back out on them."

"That's all right. I'll use the time to get the supplies we'll need and pick you up first thing Saturday morning. Say, about eight?"

"You could come over after I get home from Frank's, and we can still leave first thing in the morning."

"That's not a good idea."

"Why?"

"I'm afraid we'd never make it out of your house. What would the neighbors think?"

With that, my stomach did a double flip.

The next day and a half passed in a blur. I packed and repacked my overnight bag and worked on my new *Emily Says*. It still needed quite a bit of work, but I was anxious to get Betsy and

Joey's reaction to the story.

At first, I worried that I would be so nervous about the weekend with Gil that I wouldn't be able to concentrate on the story. I was amazed that did not seem to be the case. When I thought about it, I understood. Gil and I had been two-stepping around each other for months. We both knew it was time to move the relationship on.

Finally, Friday evening came. At 5:30 it was already pitch black, so I drove my car over to Frank's. In nice weather I would have taken the path through the pasture. It would be months before I could do that again.

Betsy and Joey were full of energy, and Betsy kept trying to convince her grandma Mildred that we should do the story before we ate. I finally told her I couldn't tell stories on an empty stomach.

Supper, as usual, was magnificent: fricassee of chicken with homemade egg noodles, green beans almandine, fresh Parker House rolls, and then to top it all off, lemon meringue pie.

"I'd weigh two hundred pounds if I let you feed me all the time," I said. "You have a real gift."

Mildred, like always, tried to brush off my praise, but I knew she was pleased. Everything she cooked was from scratch. A Stouffers package had never graced her freezer, unlike mine where the compartment held a full complement.

"Now, Jessie, now," Betsy said. "Now will you tell us the new *Emily Says*?" Joey let his older sister do most of the wheedling, but he was jumping up and down at her side.

"Okay, guys, let's go into the living room." There was a nice fire burning in the fireplace. The layout of Frank and Mildred's house was identical to mine, as was Aunt Henrietta and George's. The two brothers, George and my dad, had walked and worked in lock step through their lives. They figured if something was good enough for one member of the family, it was good enough for the rest.

"Now then, where shall we begin?" I said after we got settled on the couch.

"I know, I know, please," Betsy said. "Let me."

"Go ahead."

"Emily was sitting in the corner of her family room, reading the *Encyclopedia Britannica*. What volume is she on now, Jessie?" Betsy asked.

"She is just starting volume six."

"That's right," Betsy said, "because she was on five in *The Sunburnt Ghost*. Anyway, she was sitting there reading when her friend Karen came running into the room." Here Betsy stopped. "It's your turn now, Jessie."

I smiled and settled myself. "As you know, Karen always has problems and questions, and she comes to Emily for help. Usually it is because of something a friend has said or done, but this time it was Karen's mother who had her confused.

"Emily looked up from her book and asked what the problem was this time.

"Sometimes Emily got a little exasperated with all of Karen's interruptions," I said.

"What's exasberated mean?" Joey asked.

"Not exasberated," I said. "It's exasperated with a 'p' and it means to get angry or irritated at someone."

"Yeah, Joey, like I get when you spy on me and my friends," Betsy said.

"Her mother had said she shouldn't judge a book by its cover," I continued, "and Karen had no idea what that meant. Emily knew she'd better explain or Karen wouldn't leave her in peace, so she placed her finger in the encyclopedia to keep her place, and started her story.

"There was a little boy named Timothy Fullerton Smith, but most people called him Timmy. He was nine years old and lived with his mother and little sister in a small house on the edge of town."

"Doesn't he have a father, Jessie?" Betsy asked.

"Yes, but he's in the army, and he hasn't been home for a year."

"Not even for Christmas?"

"That's right," I said and wondered if I should put in something about armies and wars. I made a mental note to think about that later. "Shall we get back to Emily's story?"

"Yeah," Joey said. "Quit interrupting, Betsy."

I had to smile to myself. Joey, who only a year ago was happy to sit silently and defer to his sister, was starting to demand his place in the sun.

"Timmy was the smallest kid in the fourth grade and thin as a straw. He looked like a simple snap would break him in half.

"He had gotten used to being chosen last for games, but when he did play, the big boys, led by Tyler and Brandon, ganged up on him. 'Get the Shrimp,' they'd yell. If he complained, everybody laughed, even the girls, and kicked or threw the ball harder. No matter how he twisted and dodged, they hit him. He tried not to cry, but sometimes he couldn't help it, it hurt so badly. Then they'd call him 'sissy' and 'cry baby.' "

"Why are they so mean to him?" Betsy asked.

"I'm not sure," I said. "What do you think is going on?"

"I think they are showing off. They know they can beat up on Timmy because he's so little. They'd be afraid to try that with someone who was bigger than they are. What happens next?"

"There was one thing Timmy could do better than anybody else in the class and that was climb trees. Show him a tree and he'd scramble up it faster than a monkey. His favorite trees were the giant sycamores in the back of the school yard, where the drainage ditch ran, but any tree would do."

"What are sycamores?" Joey asked.

Betsy let out a sigh. "Don't you know anything?" she asked but didn't wait for an answer. "You know, the great big trees down by the creek that have the fuzzy balls on them every fall. The ones with the funny-looking bark that peels off like our skin does when we get sunburned."

Joey nodded. "What happens now, Jessie?"

"When Timmy sat in the top of one of them, he felt like the king of the world and he was sure he could see to the end of the earth. He didn't climb trees to show off. In fact, the only person who knew of his skill was a little girl in the third grade named Jenny, who lived behind the school.

"But climbing trees got lonely. Timmy desperately wanted to be part of the gang, but it seemed the harder he tried, the more he failed, no matter what the game was. There was always somebody better or faster than he was. Then came the worst day of his life."

"This is an awfully sad story, Jessie," Betsy said. "I don't see how it can have a happy ending."

Betsy did have a good point. So far it had been pretty depressing and would soon get worse. Maybe I should make it less black. "Can you be patient for a bit more?"

Betsy nodded.

"It was afternoon recess, and they were playing Cops and Robbers. Timmy was on the Robbers team and one of the first to be caught. But this day, instead of putting him in the 'jail' under the fire escape, Tyler and Brandon dragged him behind the school. 'We're going to show you what we do with shrimps,' Tyler said. 'Get the rope, Brandon.'

"Timmy struggled as hard as he could, but he was no match for Tyler and Brandon. They shoved him down on the ground, face first, and tied his hands and feet. No sooner did they have the knots tight than the bell for the end of recess rang. 'See you later, Shrimp,' they yelled as they ran away. 'Maybe this'll teach you to quit messing with the big kids.' "

"But, Jessie, did they just leave him there?" Joey asked.

"I'm afraid they did," I said.

"It wasn't till school ended for the day that the little girl, Jenny, found him as she walked home from school. She ran back and got his teacher who untied him, but when his teacher asked who had tied him up, Timmy wouldn't tell. All he said was, 'It was an accident.' That was the day Timmy decided to stop trying to be part of the gang."

"I guess he was afraid they'd really gang up on him if he tattled," Betsy said.

"One Tuesday, all the children in the fourth grade were playing kick ball during recess. All the children, that is, except Timmy. He was hiding behind the dumpster outside the cafeteria door. He had hidden behind the dumpster every recess since that horrible day."

"I'll bet it smelled stinky," Joey said. "The one at our school does."

Another item I needed to add, I thought.

"Suddenly Timmy heard loud yelling and when he popped his head up over the dumpster, he saw Tyler and Brandon, followed by the other kids, chasing a small black and white cat. Brandon was throwing rocks at her. She headed for the closest sycamore tree and scrambled up the trunk. Brandon picked up more rocks and kept throwing them, but the cat climbed out of his reach.

"The principal came out to see what was going on, so Brandon hid the rocks in his pocket. 'What's going on?' the principal asked. Before anyone else could answer, Tyler stepped forward and said, 'There's a cat in the tree. We're afraid she will fall, so we're trying to get her to come down.' "

"Tyler lied to the principal! He's going to get in big trouble," Betsy said. "It's bad to lie to your teacher, but it's even more bad to lie to the principal."

Different degrees of bad, I thought. I had to remember that and work it into the story.

" 'Why don't you try to call the cat down.' the principal said. 'I have a meeting, so I must leave, but if she's still up there when I get back, I'll call the fire department to bring a ladder.' Everybody started calling, 'here, kitty, kitty' and 'nice kitty' and 'come kitty,' but the cat wouldn't come down. In fact, she climbed higher.

" 'Maybe someone should climb up and get her,' a voice said from the back. 'Tyler, why don't you do it?' By this time the kitty was more than halfway up the tree."

"How high is that?" Joey asked.

I thought for a minute. "You know how high the cupola is on your grandpa's barn?"

Both children nodded.

"It's higher than that."

"Wow" was the response.

"Anyway, let's see what happens next," I said. "Tyler stood there looking up, not moving. Finally someone said, 'He's scared.' Tyler said, 'I'm not scared. I've got the wrong kind of shoes on. Brandon can do it.' But everybody knew the wrong kind of shoes hadn't kept him from climbing. He was scared. 'Not me,' Brandon said. 'It's too high. Besides, my mother won't let me climb trees.'

"Everybody agreed it was high and maybe they should wait for the principal to call the fire department to rescue the cat. They argued back and forth until the little girl, Jenny, stepped forward. 'Timmy can do it. I've seen him climb the tree lots of times. He'll bring the cat down.' "

Betsy and Joey were both nodding. "Timmy can do it," Joey said. "I know he can."

"Tyler and Brandon started to laugh. 'The Shrimp? He can't

even climb a staircase. He's a teeny tiny shrimp.' The other children laughed and chanted, 'Timmy's a teeny tiny shrimp.'

"Timmy walked over to the tree then backed up a few feet. He knew he had to get a running start because the first hand-hold was over his head. The kids were still laughing when he made his move, but they quickly stopped. All eyes were on Timmy as he moved smoothly up the tree. In minutes he was sitting on the tree branch next to the cat, softly stroking her and whispering in her ear.

" 'Wow! Did you see that?' someone said. 'He's so brave. He's a hero.' "

"I knew he could do it," Joey said. "He was a hero."

"From that day forward, nobody called Timmy 'Shrimp' again. He was still usually chosen last for the teams, but he didn't mind. Any time he started to feel sorry for himself, he would climb a tree and look down on the world and remember the day he was a hero. 'So see,' Emily said, 'Tyler and Brandon looked and acted big and strong, but inside they were really bullies and scaredy-cats. Timmy was little and skinny, but he was really the strong and brave one. That's what your mother meant when she said, 'You can't judge a book by its cover.' It's what's inside that determines what a person is like."

"What happened to the cat?" Betsy asked.

Hmmm, I thought to myself. *Can't forget to work that into the story.*

"The school children put up notices all over the neighborhood and went door-to-door, but they never found out who the little black and white cat belonged to. Timmy asked his mother and she said okay, so the cat became Timmy's. Because she was so little, Timmy named her Shrimp."

CHAPTER 17

The Milky Way stretched like a froth of whipped cream across the sky. Even though it was cold, I paused before I went into the house to admire the brilliant display. The town lights cast a small blur on the horizon, but the rest of the night sky glowed and pulsed against the black background. Just as I turned to go into the house, a blaze of fire streaked from east to north, a shooting star making one last statement.

The story had gone well, though it was still pretty rough. With luck I would have it ready to send off shortly after the first of the year. I didn't know who the illustrator would be. That was up to the publisher.

All the time I had been telling the story to the kids, I was nagged by the recurring feeling that the theme of Emily's story was similar to the events and people revolving around the inheritance, including Floyd's accident. Emily was correct. You can't always judge a book by its cover. I strongly suspected that I was missing something important.

Genevieve was sitting at the door. I had given up trying to understand cats. She was always waiting for me when I came home, but as soon as I walked inside, she would show me her tail end and stalk away.

The light was flashing on the answering machine, and as soon as I heard Gil's voice, all thoughts of dead bodies, inheritances, and children's stories vanished. My whole being was focused on the morning to come and thirty-six uninterrupted hours with Gil. He reiterated he would pick me up at eight. No need to call him back as he was going to bed early to make up for lost sleep.

I was out of bed before the sun was up and headed down to the kitchen with an unusually light step. No plodding for me today. Gil had assured me I only need pack for myself, he would bring everything else.

By the time the sun came over the woods, I was on my third cup of coffee. It looked to be a beautiful day, the sky cloudless. The coating of frost on the grass would soon evaporate. Promptly at eight Gil pulled into the lane. He was driving his Jeep. No patrol car. We were going to be like regular people this weekend.

The two-lane road swung away from the river. The land was still hilly, but instead of woods we drove past farms, the fields full of stubble from the harvests. We were both quiet, comfortable to watch the passing countryside without comment.

Then suddenly we were back at the river and staring down at one of the many locks and dams that controlled the navigation on the Mississippi. There were bits and pieces of ice along the edge of the water, but the channel was clear. A huge barge, heading downstream, was being locked through in sections.

A few miles further on, Gil turned off the highway onto an unmarked dirt road that stretched through an arch of leafless tree branches. I could see why he had brought the Jeep as we jolted over ruts and potholes and finally careened to a stop in front of a metal gate that was secured with a padlock. Gil hopped out and opened the padlock and within minutes we were inside the fence, the gate relocked behind us.

A few hundred feet further on, a rustic log cabin came into view. Gil stopped and pointed. "Our sanctuary for the weekend."

We quickly unloaded. It looked like Gil had brought enough

food and wine for a week. The cabin, built close to the edge of the bluff, faced west with a marvelous screened-in porch overlooking the river. The front door led into a large room with a stone fireplace across the back. A grouping of heavy wooden furniture with bright plaid upholstery faced the fire. The wooden-plank floor was covered with thick braid rugs.

"This is lovely," I said. "Who owns it?"

"A buddy of mine, Greg Porter. We were on the force together in Chicago, in the same recruit class. He inherited it from his dad. Let me give you the grand tour," Gil said with a bow.

"Behold the kitchen," he said, pointing to a galley off to the side with a counter and stools looking into the living room. "Back here," he led me through a door next to the fireplace, "the master boudoir and bath. Upstairs is a bunk room and another bath. What do you think? Is okay?"

"Is okay," I answered. "Very okay."

"Why don't you unpack the coolers while I get a fire started. Then we'll have a quick lunch, and I'll show you the rest of the property."

We walked along the bluff, inching up to the edge to look down at the river. A path zigzagged down the bluff to the water. Hand railings and stone steps had been installed at strategic spots. A small wooden dock sat at the bottom.

"Next summer we can bring my boat up here. Take us most of the day for the trip, but it is beautiful," Gil said. "And you haven't lived until you've gone through those locks in a little power boat. The only thing more exciting would be to go through in a canoe. Isn't this a great spot?"

I felt a jolt when Gil mentioned the future. I had been as- siduously avoiding thinking much beyond the next week with our relationship. Even though it had been more than two years since Alec left me, I was still gun-shy about commitment. Actually, that wasn't quite true. I had just decided not to think about it. Me and Scarlet O'Hara, I thought.

"You seem to know a lot about this place. Do you come here a lot?" I asked. *And have you brought other women here?* I thought. *Oh, Jessie,* I cautioned myself, *beware the green-eyed vixen.*

"Not as much as I used to or would like to. The first time was the summer after Elizabeth died. Megan and I came here for a couple of weeks. We both needed time to heal. Something about sitting on the porch and watching the sun set over the river helped that process. I've always been grateful to Greg for insisting we come. You're going to have to meet him. He's a great guy."

Gil didn't talk about his wife often. I knew she had died five years earlier and that was when Gil decided to move back to Riverport with Megan. Every time he mentioned her, his voice would soften. He must have loved her deeply.

The sun was starting to go down. "Let's go back, get ourselves a glass of wine, and sit on the porch," I said. "Then we can start dinner. All this fresh air has me ravenous."

Gil grilled the steaks over coals in the fireplace. We sat on the floor and ate our dinner off the coffee table in front of the fire. We both ate like we hadn't seen food for weeks.

"This soldier is dead," Gil said as he emptied the wine bottle into my glass. "Shall I open another?"

"Why not? It's Saturday night and we don't have to drive anywhere."

I took the dirty dishes to the kitchen and unceremoniously dumped them in the sink. They could wait till later. Gil moved to the couch and propped his feet on the coffee table. I plopped down next to him. "Nice fire."

Gil stared at the fire then slowly turned and looked at me. "It's not too late to stop."

"I know."

"Do you want to?"

"Stop? No." My answer came quickly even though I knew it would change our relationship forever. I had been tossing the pros and cons of sleeping with Gil back and forth for the last several months, almost since we had started seeing each other last summer. Gil gave me something I had never experienced in a relationship, certainly not what it was like with Alec. Secure and never tentative in his actions, never threatened by the actions and opinions of others. Never needing to belittle those around him to establish his superiority.

He set his glass on the table and took my hands. "Jessie, I think I'm falling in love with you. I thought you should know that."

All I could do was nod.

"I'm not asking for any kind of commitment from you," he said and stopped. "God, that sounds stilted, but you know what I mean."

I nodded again and said, "When I was a kid, my parents used to let me spread out my comforter in front of the fire. I'd sprawl for hours and watch the flames, dreaming whatever fantasy had piqued my imagination that day."

"Sounds like a good idea," he said. "Wait here."

I don't think I moved a muscle as he walked through the bedroom door and returned with the comforter. I watched as he laid it carefully on the rug. Then he walked over to me, took the glass out of my hands, set it on the coffee table, and pulled me to my feet.

"You first," he said as my fingers quickly slid his sweater over his head and undid his belt. In minutes our clothes were piled on the floor and we stood there with the firelight flickering off our bodies.

All I could feel was a vast warmth moving through me as he pulled me to the floor with him. His fingers traced careful patterns over my skin, and I felt my body arch, encouraging him to bring me close. I closed my eyes and he softly kissed each eyelid and kept murmuring, "God, you're beautiful," his voice getting huskier with each murmur.

I was aware of the fire crackling in the background as we gently melded together, and the heat moved from the fireplace to our bodies.

"Good morning, sleepy head," I said as Gil came out of the bedroom, wrapped in a worn flannel robe. "Sleep well?"

"Like a baby," he said, coming across the room to the coffee pot where I stood cradling my first cup.

"Want some?" I asked.

"First things first," he said and pulled me to him. "Did you know, you make whistling noises in your sleep?"

I leaned my head back and looked at him. "Aren't you the romantic," I said. "What happened to 'Jessie, you're wonderful' and 'How did I ever live without you'?"

"Well, that too," he said and gave me a kiss that threatened to buckle my knees.

"Enough of that," I finally said, taking a deep breath and pushing him away. "I'm starving."

Gil grinned. "Yes, ma'am. Can't have the little lady fainting from hunger. What shall it be? I'm pretty handy with a skillet."

Before I finished my second cup of coffee, Gil presented me with a steaming plate of scrambled eggs, sausage, and toast. "This looks great. Imagine, two times in one week, men have cooked breakfast for me. I could get used to this."

"Yeah, I've been wanting to talk to you about that," Gil said. "I would prefer I be the only man cooking for you."

"Are you asking me to go steady with you, at least for breakfast?"

"That would be a good start. Then maybe we could work up

to lunch and on to dinner. What do you think?"

"Throw your class ring into the deal, and I'll consider it."

Gil smiled. "Isn't this great? Breakfast together just like regular people. No murder or mayhem. Not even a fender bender or Mrs. Paulson's cat up a tree. Let's take our coffee out on the porch. Grab your coat. It's still pretty chilly."

The sun had come up over the trees behind the cabin and was glinting off the surface of the water. We could hear waves lapping against the riverbank below us, and the wooden dock groaned as it rocked up and down.

"Speaking of murder and mayhem," I said.

"Must we?"

"Briefly, I promise."

Gil did his own groaning. "Go ahead."

"Do you think you'll ever discover the identity of the body you found in the fire?"

"I already have. At least I'm ninety percent certain."

All I could do was stare at him, mouth open. "What do you mean, you already have? How?" My voice squeaked. "Why didn't you tell me? I can't believe you didn't tell me."

"If you'll recall, I was rather busy this past week. Besides, I wasn't sure you were still interested."

With that comment, I punched him in the arm, and he sloshed his coffee on his robe. "Tell me."

"You didn't have to get violent."

"You haven't seen violent if you don't hurry up and tell me."

"If you insist. Remember the plastic coin holder that was in the purse we found in the yard at Kroner's?"

The light dawned. "Fingerprints. You checked it for fingerprints. And I didn't even have to remind you."

He gave me a grin. "I'm not totally worthless at detecting. We pulled off two partials and a complete thumb. We also got a partial off the driver's license. I sent them off to the FBI lab,

155

and we got a hit."

"Is she Johanna Kroner?" I asked.

"Nope. The FBI identified her as a Ruby Holliday. Isn't that a name? Her picture matches the one on the driver's license claiming she's Johanna Kroner. She'd been arrested several times in money scams and convicted and sent to federal prison once. She was paroled about a year ago, and the feds lost track of her. The scams mostly involved elderly people, and she was the bait."

My head was spinning. The bait. Like a long-lost niece. But who else was in on the scam?

"The scenario doesn't make sense," I said. "If this Ruby person was pulling a scam on old Mr. Kroner, why was she killed? Was it because Mr. Kroner died before the scam played out? I can't imagine she was in this alone. Maybe she knew too much or was trying to get more of the take."

"Jessie."

"Yes." I looked up.

"Please don't."

Here it comes again, I thought. Don't get involved. Let the professionals handle it.

But this time Gil surprised me. "Let's pretend, at least for awhile, that all is well in the world and that the only important thing is you and me, sitting on this porch, drinking coffee, and watching the river roll by."

I couldn't help myself. I felt my eyes fill with tears. I felt like someone had grabbed me and stopped my headlong plunge into the morass. I hated to admit it, but it felt good.

"What a splendid idea," I said and reached over and took his hand.

"Maybe we should go back into the house for a bit," he said. "What do you think?"

"Another splendid idea," I said and got to my feet.

Before I could take more than two steps toward the door, a bellow came from up the road. It sounded like a bull horn. "Sheriff Keller, please come up to the gate. I have an important message for you from your office."

"What the hell? I'm going to kill that goddamned Clarence," he said as he jumped off the porch steps and stalked up the drive.

"I guess the world is back to normal," I muttered.

CHAPTER 18

Twenty minutes later we were in the Jeep and headed back south.

"I am so sorry, Jessie. Clarence panicked and called the local authorities here and had them track me down. It's my fault. I should have known better than to leave any contact information with Clarence. Next time I'll give it to the state police."

"What exactly is going on?" I asked. I was completely in the dark. Gil had come running back to the cabin and said we had to pack up immediately and get back to Riverport, and without another word had started loading up the car.

"There's been another fire."

"Where?"

"At Floyd's place. Sounds pretty serious. A neighbor driving by on his way to church called in the alarm. According to Clarence, the Chief thinks it could be arson again."

"My God, Gil, what's going on?"

"I wish I knew."

Silence descended for the rest of the trip. Gil obviously didn't want to talk and my thoughts were too jumbled to put into coherent sentences.

"Do you mind dropping me at the office, so I can get the patrol car?" Gil asked as we approached Riverport. "I'll have Clarence run me out later to pick up the Jeep."

"No problem," I said. "I'll put the food away. Maybe you'll get done in time and we can have dinner. We have more than enough leftovers."

"I have a feeling the fates will be working against us today. I'm so sorry. I thought if we left town we wouldn't be interrupted. I guess next time we'll have to leave the country."

"I'll make sure my passport's up to date," I said.

The lots and streets around the Riverport churches were packed full. A typical Sunday morning. I wondered what the congregants would say if they knew their sheriff and the girl who came back home had been engaging in carnal activity. I smiled to myself. Some would say it's about time, some could care less, and others, Aunt Henrietta came to mind, would see the fires of hell reflected in our eyes.

As Gil pulled in behind the courthouse, I reached out my hand and put it on his shoulder. "Thank you for a wonderful time," I said.

He stopped the Jeep and turned to me. "Was it okay? I mean, oh, hell, I don't know what I mean."

"Yes, Gil, it was okay. Maybe we can do it again sometime."

He grinned. "Deal," he said and hopped out. "See you later."

"Don't forget to call."

Genevieve, as usual, was waiting at the door, but this time she didn't stalk away. She stood her ground and scolded me roundly. From the tone of her voice, I was glad I didn't understand cat language.

"Well, kitty, you can scold me all you like. Nothing is going to disturb my good mood. I had a fabulous time," I said as I emptied the stale food out of her bowl and filled it with her favorite shrimp and fish gruel.

After I put the perishables away in the refrigerator, I made myself a fresh pot of coffee. The crisp sunny day matched my mood. I found myself smiling as I reviewed the past day.

Gil and I had only slightly more than twenty-four hours

together, but I knew that brief time had changed our relationship forever. A sense of comfort was replacing the edginess that had shrouded us before. He was funny and sweet, thoughtful, not to mention sexy. Oh, my God, Jessie, I thought. You sound like a love-struck teenager.

As I sat sipping my coffee, Genevieve crawled into my lap. "You are easy, my pet," I said as I rubbed her. "You'll never be a femme fatale, if you don't play hard to get." Nor will you, Jessie, I thought. But so what? Time is fleeting.

I didn't know what to make of the bombshell Gil had dropped. The body in the fire was not Johanna Kroner, as we were supposed to believe, but someone named Ruby Holliday, a scam artist well known to the federal law authorities. Instead of clarifying matters, as more events surrounding the Kroner inheritance unfolded, the more confusing it became. And where did Floyd's car crash and the fire at his place fit in? Or were they just coincidental? I didn't think so. There had to be a connection somewhere.

I suspected Patricia Fowler was a major player in the affair. She had a close relationship with the Reverend Smythe. Then there was the curious event I witnessed in the parking lot of the supermarket. Patricia by Floyd's Hummer, and him speeding off, almost bowling her over in the process. It was likely she was the catalyst in old Mr. Kroner's embracing of God's Fellowship. And then there was her genealogy expertise. I tapped my fingers on the tabletop. I'd bet the farm she's the source of the long-lost niece.

It would be interesting to talk to Patricia. Ask a few subtle questions and maybe some not so subtle. I wasn't sure how I could arrange that. Then I remembered. Reverend Smythe's address book. My plan to leave it hidden under the bed, on reflection, seemed rather stupid. I'd call her later, when I was sure she was home from church. Then it occurred that I should check the paper and see if there were any services or visitations scheduled at the mortuary. The few times I had visited the funeral home, Patricia had always been in attendance. They probably had an answering machine. Might even be better if she called me.

It was eleven o'clock. Time to kill.

"What say, Genevieve, we walk down to the mailbox and see what the mailman brought us yesterday while we were off on our rendezvous?" The question, of course, was academic. Genevieve had no intention of leaving the warm house.

The twigs scattered around the yard were all that was left from the ice storm. One of these days I would have to get out with my rake and clean them up. The mailbox was jammed with the usual assortment of catalogues. With Christmas less than six weeks away, it would get worse before it got better. Stuck in the midst of the pile was a fat envelope marked private, confidential from Scrugs and Benson Law Firm. Finally, the copy of Mr. Kroner's will. It had certainly taken them long enough.

I hurried back to the house, threw my jacket at the coat hook, poured myself another cup of coffee, and sat down at the kitchen table again. I carefully slit open the envelope and unfolded the stiff pages. They were bound together at the top. I forced myself to read all the whereases, though I was sorely tempted to skip to the meat of the document. Finally on page three it began.

"The bulk of my estate," I read out loud, "excluding payment of the additional bequests enumerated in this will, shall go to the great-great-granddaughter of Thomas Kroner, my great niece Johanna Kroner. If Johanna Kroner does not claim the inheritance within two years of my death or is declared dead, my estate shall be split evenly between my nephew Floyd T. Kroner and Reverend John W. Smythe, Jr., pastor of God's Fellowship Church or his successor, headquartered in Evanston, Illinois, to be used as he sees fit to further the expansion of his ministry

161

under the terms iterated above. One Hundred Thousand Dollars shall be set aside from my estate to reward any person or persons who provide valid information to the existence of and/or the whereabouts of Johanna Kroner. If no person has a valid claim to the reward, the One Hundred Thousand Dollars shall become a part of the estate. The validity of the claim or claims shall be determined by the Law Firm of Scrugs and Benson.

"If my nephew Floyd Kroner should predecease me or if he should die before the distribution of my estate as detailed in this document, the monies bequeathed to him, including the monies from the sale of my properties, shall be turned over to Reverend Smythe of God's Fellowship or his successor."

Oh my God, was all I could think. A better motive for murder would be hard to find. Maybe Floyd's accident hadn't been an accident. I wondered if Gil knew about this provision.

The next page held the listing of the additional bequests:

1. To my housekeeper, Lydia Dietrick, I do bequeath the sum of Two Thousand Dollars ($2,000) for her kind and faithful service over the past fifteen years.
2. To Patricia Fowler, I do bequeath the sum of Two Thousand Dollars ($2,000) to help defray her expenses as she continues her search for lost souls.

"My, my, my. Isn't that interesting," I muttered. Was old Mr. Kroner one of her lost souls?

3. To the Walnut Creek (Iowa) Historical and Genealogical Society, I do bequeath One Thousand Dollars ($1,000) in appreciation for their kind and patient assistance.

Wait a minute. Walnut Creek? Wasn't that where Patricia grew up and where Reverend Symthe's father was a pastor? I made a mental note to go back over the genealogical material I had found in the boxes Mr. Kroner left to the Spencer County Historical Society. Maybe I could do it tomorrow. This was getting more and more interesting.

4. To Jessie Schroeder who always cringed when I called her Missy, I do bequeath the sum of Five Hundred Dollars ($500) to plant lilacs in the location of her choice.

I continued to be amazed that after all these years, it was thirty by my calculation, he remembered me and the day he gave me lilacs for my mother.

I turned the pages back and reread the will. It seemed straightforward. The only real surprise was the section about Floyd. I assumed the lawyers had procedures in place to check on the authenticity of anyone who turned up claiming to be Johanna Kroner. I was beginning to suspect that there was no Johanna. If she did exist, why stage the charade at the fire scene?

I checked the time. Patricia should be home by now. Hopefully, I could catch her before they sat down for Sunday dinner. I was in luck. She answered on the first ring, almost as if she had been waiting for a call.

"Patricia, this is Jessie Schroeder. I hope this isn't a bad time."

If she was surprised to hear from me, she hid it well. She assured me the time was fine, and we chatted briefly about the weather.

"Do you know anything about how Floyd's doing?" I asked. "Last I heard he was still in a coma and going into surgery. And now with the fire at his place, the fates seem to be arranged against him."

"Floyd?" She sounded surprised to hear his name. "Oh, you mean Floyd Kroner. The last I heard was when Johnny, I mean Reverend Smythe, called from the hospital Wednesday night.

He said Floyd came through the surgery. I guess it's a waiting game now."

"Sounds like he's lucky to be alive."

"Amen to that. By the way, it was kind of you to take care of Johnny Tuesday night. He should have known better than to try to drive through the ice storm, but it was typical of him. He always puts his flock's welfare before his own."

"Good thing he saw my light. He wasn't exactly dressed to be out on a night like that."

I didn't quite know how to switch the conversation to Mr. Kroner's will. I almost dropped the telephone when she beat me to the punch.

"I am so glad you called," Patricia said. "I've been dying to hear the story behind the money Mr. Kroner left you for lilacs."

I stammered a bit while I tried to collect my thoughts. "It goes back a long way," I finally said.

"Do tell me, please."

So I told her, including the part where Mr. Kroner always insisted on calling me Missy and how mad it made me. "I'm amazed he remembered me or the time he sent me home with an armload of lilacs for my mother," I said.

Patricia sighed. "It doesn't surprise me. He was such a sweet man. I do miss him."

A sweet man! I had never heard a Kroner referred to as sweet. Even my dad said Fred Kroner could be as mean as a junkyard dog. I supposed the years may have mellowed him, but there had been a long way to go.

"I noticed that you got a nice little bequest also," I said.

"I was so surprised when I found out, you could have knocked me over with a feather." Patricia made the little simper that drove Cousin Frank nuts. "Before he died, he was always trying to reimburse me for the gas I used when I came out to see him, and, of course, I refused. I guess the bequest was his

164

way of having the last word."

Patricia seemed to be in a talkative mood, so I decided to press further. "Do you think the body was Mr. Kroner's long-lost niece?" I was pretty sure it was not common knowledge yet that the body had been identified.

"Why do you ask?" Patricia's voice grew cold.

"I don't know," I said. "It just seems terribly convenient."

"I would hardly call being burned to death 'convenient.' " If anything her voice got even colder. "I've got to go. Nice talking to you."

Nice going, Jessie, I thought. *Now you've lost her.*

"Wait a minute. Don't hang up," I said. "I almost forgot to tell you why I called. The next time you speak to Reverend Smythe, tell him he left his address book at my house. I'm sure he's missing it." *And you might ask him why my name and number are in it.*

"I will. Thank you for calling." With that, Patricia hung up.

CHAPTER 19

"Oh, damn," I muttered. "I forgot to ask her about the Walnut Creek bequest. Guess it's too late now. I doubt she'd be too happy if I called back, since she practically hung up on me."

I wandered over to the window and looked out at my garden, neatly tucked away for the winter. It would never have the grandeur it did when Mom presided over it, but I was pleased with my developing horticultural skills. I had learned that constant vigilance was needed, especially to keep the chickweed and dandelions at bay.

I actually enjoyed pulling out the chickweed. Its shallow roots sprouted at every joint and popped out with a minimum of effort. If only the ills of the world could be ripped out as easily. Dandelions were a different matter. The taproots went deep and even the most persistent digging usually failed. I could have resorted to chemicals, but somehow that did not seem fair.

Sunday dragged on and, of course, Gil did not call. The fire at Floyd's made no sense. Clarence had made it sound much more significant than it was. If Gil had known it was confined to the machine shed, he would not have felt it necessary to race back to town. The fire at old Mr. Kroner's had been set to conceal a body or, more likely, to draw attention to it. This fire destroyed nothing but farm equipment.

I debated working on my *Emily Says* revision, but I decided it was hopeless for today. My mind was too preoccupied with Gil and the strange circumstances surrounding the Kroner estate to do justice to Emily. Instead, I went to my computer and read the *New York Times,* but all that did was depress me. I finally printed out the crossword puzzle in hopes that would provide the diversion I needed. Wrong choice again. My mind seemed incapable of wrapping itself around the clues, and I quit with less than half of the squares filled in. I accepted the fact that I was getting completely wound up in the Kroner affair. The question I kept putting to myself was did my memories of the old man and his bequest for lilac bushes justify my obsession? The answer to the question was inconsequential. I was already involved.

I had learned, whenever I started putting a question over and over to myself, it was usually the first step toward figuring out what was at the root of the situation. The justification in this case could be my abhorrence of people who preyed on the lonely, many in the name of God. But, strangely, I found myself unable to hate Ruby Holliday, even though she was a bona fide member of that group. The sight of her charred arm reaching heavenward, as if beseeching, still haunted me. The fact that she died before she was incinerated was of little comfort.

Fred Kroner's bequest to the Walnut Creek Historical and Genealogical Society continued to interest me. I wondered if that was where Mr. Kroner had found out about the long-lost niece. Had Thomas Kroner settled in Walnut Creek after he abandoned his wife and sons in 1870? If so, he hadn't made it very far. But Walnut Creek was Patricia's hometown and Reverend Smythe had grown up there. Too many coincidences to suit me. I would call the Society Monday morning. Maybe I would get some answers to my questions.

Before I could analyze events further, the telephone broke my concentration. My hopes that it would be Gil were dashed as Cousin Frank's voice answered my rather breathless hello.

"Hey, Cuz, where were you last night? Your house was dark."

"Not that it's any of your business, but Gil and I decided to get away from the prying eyes of Riverport."

"Figured as much. Good time?"

"Yes, until Gil got called back early because of the fire at Floyd Kroner's place. At the rate it's going, all the Kroner farms are going to be nothing but piles of ashes."

"I hadn't heard about that. What happened?"

"The machine shed went up in flames. One of the neighbors discovered it as he was on his way to church this morning. I guess all the equipment inside was destroyed. The report said arson was suspected."

"I doubt that," Frank said. "I know a lot of people hate Floyd's guts, but why deliberately burn up machinery and a building he's probably got insured to the hilt? I wouldn't have put it past Floyd to set fire to it himself to collect the insurance, but he's tucked away in the hospital in Springfield."

"I agree," I said. "It doesn't make sense."

"I betcha' they'll find out it was an accident. I've been in that shed, and it's a mess. I don't know who did the electrical, probably Floyd himself, but there were wires and cords going every which way and he had lumber scraps and cans of fuel and paint stacked around. All it'd take was one hungry rat chewing on a cord and, poof, up it'd go."

"I guess we'll find out soon enough. You going to tattle on me?" I couldn't resist the question.

"Naw. I learned my lesson. You're a big girl. It's about time you had some fun," he said.

"Well, that's a change in attitude."

"Not really. All I did was mention that I'd seen Gil's patrol car the other night in your drive. Henrietta and George were the ones who jumped to conclusions."

Frank was probably correct, but I hated to let him off the hook so easily.

"Okay, just this once I'll accept your explanation," I said, "but you owe me."

"Fair enough. Say, this thing with Gil, is it getting serious?"

"Don't ask me that," I said. "It's too soon. We're still getting to know each other."

"Hell, Jessie, you've known Gil Keller since high school. What's to get to know?"

Frank was right. I had known Gil since high school when he was the captain and star of everything in his class. I, on the other hand, had been just one more in the adoring masses.

"Come on, Frank. People change. I'm not going to rush it this time. I learned my lesson with Alec."

"Well, if you'd asked me, I would have told you that Alec was a jerk from the beginning. He didn't change. He's still a jerk."

"Yeah, well, let's not go there," I said. "I gotta go. I'll probably talk to you tomorrow. Hi to Mildred."

I rummaged around in the refrigerator and got out a chunk of cheese and a stick of salami. I whittled off several slices of each, piled it on my plate, and added some crackers and grapes. I opened a bottle of wine and poured myself a glass. Somehow it did not exude the romantic flavor it had at yesterday's lunch. Maybe Gil would come by and help me finish it, though I doubted he would make it. The whole affair at the cabin was starting to feel more like a dream than reality.

I took my plate into the living room and stared at the television as I thought about the day with Gil and wondered what was going to happen with our relationship. He was obviously much more ready for a commitment than I was. At least that was what he professed. But did he really mean it?

Stop it, Jessie, right this minute. Gil Keller is the best thing to come along for you in a long time. Just let it take its natural course. Don't try to second guess his every word and action. If it goes, great. If not . . . there I stopped. I didn't want to go any further.

I finally took my dishes to the kitchen, rinsed them, and stuck them in the dishwasher. Tomorrow I would call Walnut Creek and see what, if anything, I could find out about the information or research they may have helped Fred Kroner with. And if time allowed, I'd get back to work on *Emily Says*.

My first look out the window at the grim, gray November morning was enough to send me straight back to my warm bed. But it was not to be, because Genevieve had taken up her post outside my door. Try as I might, her complaining and scratching could not be ignored. I pulled on a pair of wool socks and my velour sweat suit. A cold bedroom made for great sleeping, but it was hell getting up in the mornings.

I went through my morning routine—cat first, then me. I was halfway through my bowl of cereal (with sliced banana) when the phone rang.

"Good morning, sunshine." It was Gil.

"You sound chipper this morning," I said. "No more crises on the home front?"

"Nope. And the one existing crisis is no more. The arson boys took one look at the fire scene at Floyd's and pronounced it accidental."

"Doesn't surprise me. Frank told me that shed was a fire waiting to happen. I don't envy the insurance company having to deal with Floyd," I said.

"Yeah, well, it's going to be up to Floyd's estate to deal with the insurance company. Got word about an hour ago that Floyd didn't make it."

I was stunned into silence. This couldn't be.

"Jessie, you still there?"

"Are you saying that Floyd Kroner is dead?"

"Evidently the head injuries were so massive, he was brain dead. The surgery was for naught. The amazing thing is that he had signed a donor card, so lots of people are going to get a second lease on life because of Floyd Kroner. Who would have thought?"

Who would have thought? I repeated silently.

"Well, I gotta go. Thought you should know."

"Wait, wait. Don't hang up," I said. "Is there going to be an autopsy?"

"It's routine when alcohol is suspected of being a causative factor. Why do you ask?"

I told Gil about the provision in the will stating that Reverend Smythe got the whole estate if Floyd died.

"Pretty convenient, don't you think, that someone who wasn't a known drinker decides to get drunk and then go driving, during an ice storm, down a steep hill that leads straight into the bay? Think about it," I said. "If there is no Johanna and Floyd is dead, the reverend gets the whole kit and caboodle."

There was silence on the other end of the telephone, then a sigh. "Jessie, please, this is no time for conspiracy theories. Now, I do have to go. I'll call later."

I stared at the phone for a few minutes and then slammed it down with maybe a little bit more force than necessary. Conspiracy theories my foot! We'll just see about that.

I picked up the phone again and dialed Iowa information, but there was no listing for the Walnut Creek Historical and Genealogical Society. I was about to hang up when it occurred to me that someone at the public library could probably help me. I was thwarted again as I got a recorded message telling me the library was closed on Mondays and would reopen at nine A.M. on Tuesday.

Closed on Mondays! What if a person had a literary crisis on Monday?

Stop being cute, I chided myself. Let's figure out what we are going to do in the meantime.

I decided to be domestic for a change. There was laundry to be done, not to mention the thick layers of dust that covered most of the horizontal surfaces in the house. I would use the time to ponder my revisions to the Emily story.

By midafternoon the domestic urges had been extinguished, and I knew where I was going with Emily. I also had to double-check that I had used all the vocabulary words the publisher wanted included.

I brewed myself some fresh coffee and sat down to think about the Kroner mess again. I no longer considered it a mystery. It was a pure and simple mess. In a mystery, clues slowly converged on a conclusion. In this case, each new incident seemed to lead farther away from a conclusion.

I rummaged around in my desk and found the notes I had made from my search of the boxes that had come from old Mr. Kroner. Box number one had yielded nothing of interest. Boxes two through five had a few items of importance, mostly in reference to the history of Spencer County, plus the pamphlet about God's Fellowship and the confirmation Bible. But virtually nothing to do with Kroner family genealogical research. Why was that? Suddenly I sat bolt upright, upsetting Genevieve who took a flying leap off my lap. Wilma had said there were six boxes. I had only looked through five. It was almost four o'clock. I had to go to the post office and get stamps, but then I would go to the courthouse and find that sixth box.

The line was long at the one open window. I never understood why as the line got longer, the clerk moved more slowly and deliberately. I started to leave. I'd get my stamps out of the machine in the lobby. Then I noticed Patricia Fowler at the end of the line.

"Hi, Patricia," I said. "How are you today?"

She jerked toward me, and the expression on her face was less than welcoming.

"I hope you didn't mind me calling you yesterday," I said and continued, not giving her a chance to answer me. "Isn't it terrible about poor Floyd? Such a loss."

"What about Floyd?" she asked.

"He passed away this morning." At this statement, the whole line, all of whom had been listening, turned around. A collective gasp showed they had heard.

"I guess the head injuries were so massive he never had a chance. I do hope Reverend Smythe was with him."

"I'm sure he was," Patricia said.

She obviously was not going to say any more. "Will you make sure the reverend knows about Floyd, in case he wasn't there?" I said. "Oh, and don't forget to tell him he left his address book at my house."

With that statement, there was another collective gasp from the line.

"I think I'll get my stamps from the machine," I said to the group in general. "I want to get to the courthouse before it closes so I can finish my inventory of the material Fred Kroner left to the Historical Society." Why I felt the need to explain my departure, I don't know.

Gil's parking space behind the courthouse was empty. I left my car over on the side and hurried to catch Virginia before she left for the day.

"Hi there, Ms. Schroeder," she said as I came into the area where she presided over the Sheriff's Department and the Volunteer Fire Department office needs. "What can I do for you?"

"I need the key to the Historical Society storeroom again."

She opened the drawer under the counter and pulled out the big brass key and a flashlight. "I gotta leave in a few minutes, so just put them in the drawer when you finish."

"Is the Sheriff coming back in?" I asked.

"I'm not sure. Clarence is on duty tonight. Sheriff had to go to Springfield. Something about the autopsy on Floyd Kroner. You want me to leave a note in his box?"

"No, that's okay. Enjoy your evening."

I made my way down the back stairs and flipped on the light switch at the foot of the steps. If anything, it was colder and drearier than the last time I was there. I unlocked the door and started to put the key in my pocket.

"Damn," I said out loud. I had managed to wear my only pair of warm slacks that didn't have pockets. Nor did the sweat-shirt I wore over my turtleneck. Nothing to do but leave it in the lock. It didn't matter. I wasn't going to be here long. I shone the flashlight toward the ceiling to find the string that turned on the bulb that hung down in the center of the room. There were the five boxes I had gone through lined up against the south wall. Only when I looked carefully did I see the remaining carton against the back wall.

I dragged it out so it was under the light and pulled out another carton to use as a seat. The air coming in the door felt like it was straight from the North Pole, so I pulled the door closed. There was no knob or handle on the inside, but as long as the lock was not engaged from the outside, the door opened with a push. Taking a deep breath, I picked open the knot in the twine and folded the flaps back. At first glimpse, the contents looked much the same as what had been crammed into the other boxes, but I forced myself to take the items out one at a time.

About halfway through the carton, I found a manila envelope addressed to Fred Kroner c/o Patricia Fowler. The return address was the Walnut Creek Historical and Genealogical Society, Walnut Creek, Iowa. I emptied the contents out on the floor.

There were several charts covered with writing. As I squinted to see what they said, I heard a scraping at the door and footsteps. I jumped up and ran over to the door, but when I pushed, it refused to move. I reached into my pocket to get the key, but it was not there. I had left it in the outside lock. And Virginia had said it was the only key.

I yelled and pounded on the door, but there was no answer. Instead, the crack of light that had been shining under the door from the hallway went out.

CHAPTER 20

I stood there and stared at the door. I guess I thought if I looked at it hard enough, it would open. No such luck.

Now what? I felt a bubble of panic begin to form at the back of my throat. I pounded on the door with my fist.

"Hello," I yelled. "Can anybody hear me? I'm in the storeroom."

Again nothing. I leaned my head against the door, my breath coming in gasps. Someone had deliberately locked me in and turned off the hall light. Why? The grate in the door was covered from the outside. When I stuck my finger through and pushed on it, it was obvious it also was locked tight. Who, besides Virginia, even knew I was down here? Then I remembered. Patricia Fowler and the rest of the people in line at the post office. But why would she or somebody else even bother? It was a little late to be posing that question. Someone had.

I sat back down on the box. Stupid, stupid, stupid to leave the key in the lock. Thank God, the ceiling light was not connected to the hall switch. I looked at my watch. Six o'clock. I wondered how long it would take me to die of starvation and/or dehydration. Days? Weeks? Hours?

For God's sake, stop it, I told myself. You're in the basement of the courthouse. It's not like you're in an abandoned house in the middle of nowhere. If not before, someone will find you in the morning. The lecture did nothing to still my pounding heart.

I rummaged through my purse. A box of tic tacs, an energy

bar stiff with age, and some cough drops that had fused to their wrappers. Then in the bottom I discovered my cell phone. My elation was short lived. When I turned it on, the only thing it registered was "no service." What did I expect? I was in a basement room with two-foot thick stone walls.

The papers I had dumped out of the envelope were scattered around the floor. I scooped them up into a pile and flipped through them. Several had been neatly bound together with a cover page entitled, Genealogical Chart, Numbers 1 through 3, Johanna Elizabeth Kroner, born June 4, 1971, in Des Moines, Iowa. Prepared for Fred T. Kroner.

Prepared for Fred T. Kroner, but prepared by whom. Did the folks in Walnut Creek do the research? Is that why he left them $1,000? Or was it someone else? Maybe our own genealogical expert Patricia? Damn, I needed to talk to the people in Walnut Creek. I had a feeling they held the key.

I turned back the cover page and looked at the top chart. I would have expected the great-great-grandfather, Thomas Kroner, to be in space number one, but instead it was Johanna. How could the preparer start with her when no one knew she existed? Maybe he did start with Thomas, but the accepted form of the genealogical chart was to put the most recent person in first once the lineage was established.

I looked at my watch again. Barely thirty minutes had passed. It was going to be a long night. I was starting to feel claustrophobic. I had never been good in closed spaces. I forced myself to continue looking at the papers. Maybe they would divert me.

The other two charts traced the family back even further. Seemed like superfluous research, if all that was wanted was proof of Johanna's existence. I looked at the first chart more closely. There was a notation that Thomas had married a Stella Parsons in July 1871. Why that old devil. He was a bigamist. I'll bet Stella didn't know about the wife and family Thomas left behind in Illinois.

There were other papers, mostly handwritten notations about births, deaths, and marriages, some with sources noted but mainly unsubstantiated. One Xerox, almost unreadable, looked like a family record, probably from a Bible. It looked pretty sloppy and amateurish to me, but maybe this was the way it was done. As I looked at the material, it occurred to me that there must be thousands of Kroners in the country, maybe even hundreds in Iowa alone. It wouldn't be difficult to substitute one Kroner family for another.

Poor old Mr. Kroner. I suspected he was so desperate for the niece to exist that he accepted the information without question. What role had Patricia played in all this and why?

Another half an hour had gone by. It was getting chilly in the storeroom. At least it was dry. Why hadn't I worn my parka? My nose was beginning to drip from the cold. I popped a couple of tic tacs. Maybe they would take my mind off my growling stomach. I tried to make myself as comfortable as possible. Sitting on the floor was not an option. That would be like sitting on an ice floe. I dragged a smaller carton across the room and pushed it up against one of Mr. Kroner's boxes to make myself a cardboard chair.

I had been in stupid situations before, but this had to rank at the top. Why would anyone bother to lock me in? Was it a warning? But why warn me? I had been circumspect with my inquiries. In fact, I had made only a few. No more than what other people were making. I certainly had not been rushing around town interrogating all interested parties. Maybe it was a practical joke. That was such an outlandish thought, I discarded it immediately.

The hands on my watch crept around so slowly, I kept tapping it to make sure it was working. Even the second hand seemed to be going at half speed. Periodically I would get up and stomp around my cell to get the circulation going in my feet again. Each time I passed the door, I gave it a kick. Didn't do any good, but it made me feel better. By 8:30 I had exhausted my supply of tic tacs and was beginning to eye the energy bar. Not a good idea, I decided. It would only make me thirstier.

As I looked around, I thought about the other people who had spent time in this very room. Most of them involuntarily like me. The courthouse had been built in the 1800s, and the basement level had held the jail cells. About twenty years ago, the county was ordered by the state to provide more humane quarters for the prisoners. That was when the addition was put on the back to house a new jail and space for the Spencer County Volunteer Fire Department.

I reversed my position, straddling the small box and folding my arms on the taller one to make a resting place for my head. I debated turning off the overhead light, but decided that was not wise. If someone did come looking for me, the light leaking under the door into the hall would alert him.

As soon as I put my head down, the tears started. I had run out of my supply of valor. I could only be brave for so long. I was cold and hungry and confused. Why wasn't someone looking for me? I closed my eyes and muttered a plea. "Please. Please. Please."

I don't know how long I stayed in that position. I must have drifted off, because I dreamt someone was calling my name. I raised my head in time to see the door swing open, and Gil step into the room.

"What in the hell is going on?" Gil walked across the room, wrapped his arms around me, and lifted me to my feet.

"I don't know." I buried my face in his shoulder. "I was looking through this box of papers, I guess I left the key in the outside of the door, and someone locked me in and turned off the hall lights. I didn't do anything."

"Let's get out of here," Gil said. "I've been worried out of my mind. I stopped at your place on my way in from Springfield. You weren't home, so I called your phone and left a message to call me. Then I called your cell and again no answer, so I left another message."

"How did you figure out where I was?"

"I decided to come by the office, and your car was parked out back. I had no idea why it was there, so I called your cousin Frank, but he had no idea what was going on."

"We better call him," I said, "or he'll have the militia out looking for me."

"Jessie, I am the militia. Anyway, I knew you had been poking around in some things in the Historical Society storeroom. I thought maybe you had decided to have another look, but the key was in the drawer where Virginia keeps it, and the lights were off in the basement."

We had reached the top of the stairs when I remembered. "I forgot Virginia's flashlight. We need to go back for it."

"Tomorrow will be soon enough," Gil said. "That flashlight is why I knew where to find you."

"I don't understand."

"I talked to Virginia. Had a hellava time tracking her down since this is her bingo night, but when I did, she said you'd come in late afternoon, about four-thirty, and she'd given you the key and a flashlight and asked you to put them back when you finished."

"So?"

"So I went back to the drawer. The key was there like before, but no flashlight. Jessie, I've gotten to know you pretty well. I was sure that your compulsive nature would not have permitted you to return the key, but not the flashlight. So I got the key, came downstairs, and eureka, there you and the flashlight were."

We made it to Gil's office, and I plopped down in the arm chair in front of his desk. "Gil, what is going on? Nothing makes sense—the fire, the body, Floyd's accident and death, a mysterious niece, and old Mr. Kroner's crazy will and God's Fellowship. And nothing seems to be connected. Now someone has locked me in the Historical Society storeroom. Can you explain?"

"No, but can you explain how you let yourself get locked in?"

"Stupidity. Sheer stupidity. I didn't have a pocket to put the key in, so I left it in the outside lock. You know those doors have no key holes or handles on the inside, and I didn't want to just leave it on the floor."

He looked at me for a long time. "Oh, Jessie, I should have known you would get involved."

"But, Gil, I haven't."

"I know that's what you think, but evidently you've done or said something that pushed a hot button. Who knew you were going to be in the storeroom?"

I told him about the conversation I had with Patricia at the post office. "I can't imagine she would do it, too obvious, but I guess she could have told somebody."

"Who else was there?"

"I didn't pay any attention," I said. "There were four or five other people in line."

"You hungry?"

"I'm starving. The only thing I've had to eat since lunch is half a box of tic tacs."

"How about if we go to Smitty's for some barbecue?"

My mouth started to water at the thought of Smitty's barbecue. Even in the winter, he fired up his barrel cooker a couple of times a week and smoked a half dozen pork shoulders until the meat was falling off the bone. Sweet and succulent and slathered with Smitty's secret sauce.

"Come on. We'll take the patrol car," Gil said. "It's good to remind the patrons of Smitty's occasionally that the law is keeping an eye on them."

There were an amazing number of cars in the parking lot, considering it was a cold Monday night. A couple of the customers yelled, "Hey, Sheriff, how's it doing?" when we walked in. All they did was stare at me.

Smitty was in his usual place, perched on a stool behind the bar. "What'll it be, Sheriff?" he asked as we walked by.

"Bring us two barbecue plate specials. She'll take a draft and I'll have a Coke."

We took a booth toward the back. The wooden booths and tables were covered with checkered cloths. In the middle of each sat a caddy loaded with barbecue sauce, vinegar, catsup, mustard, and several brands of hot sauce.

"I don't think I thanked you for rescuing me," I said. "Kind of romantic, like the brave knight saving the princess from the witch's tower, except I was in the basement. Anyway, thank you. I knew someone would find me, but I was getting pretty scared, not to mention hungry and thirsty."

I looked over at the bar in time to see Smitty take the tray of food and drinks from the waitress and head toward our table. "Now that's something you don't see often," I said. "Smitty getting off his stool."

"Here you go, Sheriff, Miss. Enjoy." He stood there for a minute, and then, as if making up his mind, reached behind him and pulled a chair from a nearby table over to the end of our booth and sat down.

"I heard Floyd didn't make it," he said.

"That's right," Gil said. "He passed this morning."

"He could be a mean critter," Smitty said, "but I'm sorry to hear that."

"Yeah," Gil said around a bite of barbecue.

"Thought you should know, Sheriff, that Floyd was in here the day of the ice storm before he had his accident."

Gil put down his fork. "And?"

"Well, he was with some fellow I never seen before. Didn't get a real good look at him, but he was wearing a Cubs baseball cap and had his arm in a sling."

"How many drinks did you serve them?" Gil asked.

"Just one round, and Floyd didn't even finish his. But they must've stopped someplace before they got here, because Floyd was having trouble staying on his feet when they left."

CHAPTER 21

That information was enough to make me put down my fork also.

"You ever know Floyd to drink too much?" Gil asked.

"No, not even when someone else was buying," Smitty said.

"I have to ask you why you let him go without making sure that he wasn't going to drive?" Gil asked.

Smitty shrugged. "I figured the other guy was going to drive 'cause he had the keys, and he looked okay. Besides, the weather was getting so bad, I was closing up shop. Anyway, I thought you should know."

With that, Smitty heaved himself up and shuffled back to his perch behind the bar.

"What're you going to do now?" I asked.

"Think I should put out an APB for a guy with a sling and wearing a Cubs baseball cap?" Gil grinned at me.

"No need to be a smart ass," I said. "The least you could do is make inquiries."

"Sorry. I thought I was being funny. Don't worry, I'll get Smitty in to give me a full description and find out who else was in the bar that night. Now, why don't we finish our food? You must be exhausted."

On that score, Gil was correct. I could barely keep my head out of my plate of barbecue. "I think I need to go home," I said. "Can you take me back to my car? Oh, and don't forget to get Virginia's flashlight out of the storeroom."

"I'll follow you home and make sure you get tucked in safely," Gil said.

"Fine, but don't plan on anything else."

I spent the night being buried alive, imprisoned in elevators, and lost in abandoned mines. When I woke up, I was nearly as tired as when I went to bed, and my covers were twisted into knots. I dragged myself downstairs and brewed an extra strong pot of coffee. Genevieve would have to wait. For once, she knew enough to keep her mouth shut.

As I thought back on the experiences of the previous day, they had an almost surreal quality. Floyd dies and I get locked in a basement storeroom at the courthouse. Then I remembered. I had left all the Kroner genealogy papers behind. I had a feeling they were important. Much as I didn't want to go back to the storeroom, I needed to retrieve them. I wanted to show them to someone who was well versed in genealogy research techniques. But first things first. The call to Walnut Creek.

Of course, I couldn't remember where I had written the telephone number for the library. I rummaged through the pile of papers and note cards on the corner of my desk. Some day you have to get organized, I thought. Maybe tomorrow.

I finally located the number, written on the back of the return envelope for my electric bill. Which reminded me it was time to pay bills. That was one of the few things I missed about Alec. He had handled the bill paying and finances in our marriage. There was never a missed payment or service charge when he was in charge. Of course, that was also one of the problems. He always had to be in charge.

The phone was answered on the second ring by a perky voice that identified herself as Ramona. How anyone could be perky at nine o'clock in the morning was beyond me. I identified myself and explained I was trying to get in touch with someone

185

from the Historical and Genealogy Society.

"I certainly can help you with that, dearie. I'm quite active in HAGS," she said.

"Hags?"

She laughed. "That's shorthand, you know, an acronym, for the Society. H for historical, A for and, G for genealogy, and S for society. We thought it was kind of cute to call ourselves the HAGS."

I wondered if everybody in Walnut Creek had this peculiar a sense of humor.

"Oh, I see," I said, deciding to play along. "Cute."

"Now then, what can I do for you?"

"I'm trying to track down the person who did some genealogy work for Patricia Fowler on the descendents of a Thomas Kroner who lived in the Walnut Creek area in the late 1800s."

"You mean Patsy Wiseman. Patsy and I went to school together, though, actually, she was a couple of years behind me. Hadn't heard hide nor hair from her in years, not since she married that mortician fellow and moved to Riverport. Could have knocked me over with a feather when she called. Felt real bad that we couldn't supply her with the information she needed," Ramona said.

"I beg your pardon," I said. "I thought you sent her an envelope full of information on Thomas Kroner."

"No, no. That was about a Theodore Kromer with an M," she said.

"I don't understand." That was an understatement, if there ever was one.

"Can you hold on for a minute?" Ramona asked. "I have to check someone out."

"No problem," I said, getting more confused by the minute. I was beginning to appreciate how Alice must have felt when she fell down that rabbit hole.

Finally, she was back. "Sorry about that," she said. "Now about Kroner vs. Kromer."

I was distracted for a minute, because all I could think of was the movie, *Kramer vs. Kramer*.

Ramona continued. "The Kromers have lived in and around Walnut Creek since the 1830s, but no Kroners. As you can imagine, Patsy was disappointed when I told her, but I have to give her credit. She asked me to send the Kromer information to her. She said she could use it in a class she was going to teach on pitfalls in genealogical research. She even offered to pay."

"I bet you were surprised when you were notified that a Fred Kroner had left HAGS a thousand dollars."

"Were we ever. I even called Patsy and asked her how come. She said he was appreciative of our work that had cleared up some inheritance questions for him. Seemed kind of strange, but I know better than to look a gift horse in the mouth."

"Thank you for your kindness," I said. It was time to get back to the storeroom and collect those papers.

"Wait a minute," she said. "You did say your name is Jessie Schroeder, didn't you?"

"Yes, that's my name."

"Are you by any chance the Jessie Schroeder who writes the *Emily Says* books?"

Again, I had to confess.

"Oh, my God!" She practically shrieked in my ear. "Wait till I tell the others. *Emily Says* is one of the most popular series in the Children's Section. Is there a new one in the works? The children keep asking."

"Valentine's Day is the release date for the next one."

"What's the title?"

"*Emily Says: Of Course Ghosts Get Sunburnt.*"

"We'll get it preordered. Such a thrill to talk with you."

187

"Thank you again and goodbye," I said, quickly hanging up before Ramona could get more conversation in.

I popped half an English muffin in the toaster to eat in the car on my way back to the courthouse. Probably drip butter on myself, but that was okay. I was in a hurry. I didn't want anyone getting to those papers before I did. I wondered why Patricia had deliberately misled Mr. Kroner.

I was driving myself nuts with all the "what ifs." It was time I got serious about examining the strange occurrences in an organized fashion instead of flailing around haphazardly. Either that or chuck the whole affair and get on with my life. Even before I finished the thought, I knew which way I would go.

Virginia was back on her stool.

"Oh, Ms. Schroeder, I am so sorry," she said. "Sheriff told me what happened last night. I blame myself. I was so anxious to get to bingo that I neglected my duty."

"Why in the world would you blame yourself?" I asked.

"I should have come down to tell you I was leaving. Then I would have seen the key in the lock and given it to you. You poor thing. Let me tell you. The Sheriff is furious. I've never seen him so mad. He'll find out what's going on and take care of it. What kind of warped person would do a thing like that?"

I shrugged. "I don't know, but may I have the key and flashlight again? I left some papers in the storeroom."

"Want me to come with you?" Virginia asked.

It was tempting, but I said no and headed back downstairs alone.

The storeroom was as I had left it, and I placed the key securely in my pocket. I quickly gathered up the papers scattered around the floor. I'd wait till I got home to examine them. I was not going to stay in that room one second longer than I needed. I did force myself to slow down and make sure I had everything out of the sixth box that I needed. I stuffed the collection into a manila folder, locked the door, returned the key and flashlight, and headed home. As far as I was concerned, that would be my last visit to the Historical Society storeroom.

I cleared the dining-room table and spread out the contents of the envelope. Most of the papers were photocopies of original documents, some with handwritten notations. I picked up what appeared to be a baptismal certificate. The name, recorded on it in an elaborate script, was blurry. I got out my magnifying glass and looked it over. As best I could decipher, it said "Bernard Henry Kroner, son of T. Kroner and S. Parsons Kroner, accepts the word of God this Fifteenth Day of July, Eighteen Hundred and Seventy Two."

In each name the *n* was barely legible, and it looked to my untrained eye that it took up more space than it should. I couldn't swear to it yet, but I would bet good money that someone had tampered with the names, the most likely candidate being Patricia Fowler.

Next was a photocopy of a picture of a double tombstone. The family surname was chiseled across the top of the marker. The copy was so fuzzy that the name could have been Kroner or Kromer. Below the surname the message "Into Your Hands We Commend These Thy Servants" followed by Bernard Henry, 1872–1923, and Patience Agnes, 1880–1936.

Two more blurry photos of grave sites had notations on the back. One claimed to be the final resting place of a Franklin G. Kroner, 1910–1973, and the other of an Edward F. Kroner, 1941–1987. The piece de resistance was a photocopy of a birth certificate for Johanna Ellen Kroner, born June 4, 1969. Again, all the *n* letters were quite blurred and could have been *m*.

I pushed back my chair and walked over to the dining-room window. There was nothing remarkable out there, just another gray and dreary November day. But the picture in my mind's eye was starting to clear. There was no Johanna, probably never

189

had been. Poor Mr. Kroner, his old eyes wouldn't have been able to pick up on the altered papers. The whole thing had been a ruse.

Of course, that didn't explain why a body with false papers identifying her as Johanna was found at the fire. Why go to the trouble? Unless there was some kind of a double-cross under way. I rubbed my temples with my fingers. This was getting me nowhere. Maybe I should turn the papers over to the lawyers or, better yet, let Gil handle it.

But before I did that, I felt it important to confront Patricia and tell her I knew what she had done. It needed to be handled in person, not on the telephone. I owed that much to Mr. Kroner and his $500 for lilacs.

CHAPTER 22

I needed to figure out exactly how I was going to approach Patricia. It was important that I make it a surprise visit. I didn't want her to have time to muster her defenses. None of the previous occasions when I talked with her had gone well, particularly the phone call I made about the reverend's address book.

What did I know about Patricia? She grew up in Walnut Creek, Iowa, and she and the Rev. John W. Smythe, Jr., had a long history together, going back to childhood. The reverend had introduced her to Sheldon. A curious trio. I knew the relationship each man had with Patricia, but what I had yet to discover was the exact relationship between the two men. Were they just good friends or was there more?

Patricia was a major recruiter for God's Fellowship in Spencer County, successful with Mr. Kroner, not successful with Mildred. The two cases I was familiar with. She was also the supposed expert of genealogical research in the area. She was likely the person who had persuaded old Mr. Kroner that he had a long-lost niece named Johanna. Was it an honest mistake on her part that she confused Kroner with Kromer? I very much doubted it.

What to say to her? I waited for a flash of inspiration, but none was forthcoming, and I doubted any kind of flash was going to occur. "Oh, hell, Jessie," I muttered to myself. "Just wing it." I changed into clothing more appropriate for visiting a mortuary and headed into the center of town.

Fowler's Funeral Home was an elegant structure, a two-story red brick with heavy white carved wooden trim. A portico stretched across the front supported by white pillars that rose out of a brick planter. In the summer the planter was ablaze with red and white geraniums. Now it contained a layer of evergreen boughs. The driveway under the portico swung past double doors through which the caskets were rolled into the waiting hearses.

The parking area on the side looked to be freshly black topped, each parking space etched in crisp white lines. Only the blue diagonal lines and symbols of the handicapped spaces marred the perfect symmetry.

I pulled my car into a space next to the building. Mine was the only car in the lot. I sat for a moment and took a deep breath before I climbed out. As I turned away from my car, I heard a door slam, an engine rev, and wheels screech. A large black sedan came careening out of the drive behind the mortuary. It was hard to see through the tinted glass, but it looked to be Sheldon Junior at the wheel. I guessed that big black sedans were part of the dress code for funeral directors. I raised my hand in greeting, but he was looking neither right nor left as he sped past me. The car skidded as he made a sharp right turn and accelerated up the street.

Someone seems upset, I thought. Wonder what's got him going? I'd never known Sheldon to lose his cool. In fact, he rarely showed any kind of emotion.

A soft chime sounded as I opened the door into the funeral home. The thick carpeting threatened to swallow my shoes and made walking difficult, like wading through sand. I was no more than a half dozen steps down the hall when Sheldon Senior popped into view.

"Miss Schroeder, how nice to see you," he said, hand

extended. "What brings you to our abode? Not business, I hope."

He was a larger version of his son, his body big-boned and rotund whereas his son's was sculpted and trim. His rosy cheeks made me wonder if he had a fondness for the bottle, a weakness for which I could hardly blame him. But then again, it could have been the fumes that permeated the air in the room downstairs.

"I'm looking for Patricia. Is she here?"

"She's upstairs in the residential quarters. Take those stairs in the back and go on up. Just give a knock on the door."

"Thank you," I said, thinking that had been easy.

"Terrible about Floyd," he called after me.

I stopped and turned. "Yes. A lesson for all of us to wear our seat belts."

"Amen to that. Good to see you."

The carpet became much more utilitarian as I approached the residential quarters. There was something perverse about spending more lavishly on the dead than on the living.

I pushed the doorbell and waited. Nothing. I pushed it again and gave a rap on the door with my knuckles. I thought I heard soft footsteps then a quiet voice inquired, "Who is it?"

"It's Jessie Schroeder. I need to talk to you."

"Go away."

That was not the answer I expected, and it stopped me for a minute. "No, I won't," I said. "I'm staying here until you let me in." I guess that was a bit cheeky of me, but there was no way Patricia was going to put me off. I knocked again.

A few minutes later the door opened. Patricia stood there, looking like a housewife's nightmare in a flowered muumuu and dirty terry cloth scuffs, her hair askew.

But the thing that grabbed my attention was her puffy eyes and tear-streaked cheeks.

"What do you want?" she asked in a monotone.

"Are you all right?" I stepped into the vestibule and gently placed my hand on her arm.

She recoiled as if I had touched her with a hot poker, and grabbed a wad of tissues out of her pocket. "What do you want?" she repeated between teary gulps into the Kleenex.

"Here, let's sit down and I'll fix you a cup of tea," I said and led her into the living room. I could smell the booze on her breath. Lord knows how much she had had, but maybe the tea would help neutralize it.

Patricia collapsed onto the sofa and proceeded to sob.

I went into the kitchen and looked in vain for tea bags and finally settled on a glass of water. At the rate she was weeping, she would need rehydrating.

"Here drink this and tell me what's wrong," I said and sat down beside her.

She looked at me over the sodden mass of tissues and wailed, "He said I was a meddling, incompetent fool. He said it was all my fault."

"Who?" I asked though I was sure I knew. That had been an angry man who passed me in the parking lot, but I wanted to hear her say it.

"Junior, that's who. He yelled at me." With that she grabbed another handful of tissues.

"Want to talk about it?"

"Yes. No. It's too personal."

She huddled in the corner of the sofa, folded in on herself. All I could do was wait.

Patricia finally shook her head and in a whisper I could barely hear, she said, "He didn't have to tell me. And that awful Floyd. He didn't have to tell me, either. Before I could pretend. Now he's made it real."

"What's real?" I asked.

At my question Patricia raised her head and stared at me, puzzled, as if she had just become aware that I was sitting next to her. "What are you doing here?

"I came to talk to you. Let me get you another glass of water."

"Yes, water. That's what I need."

As I ferried another eight ounces of water back to Patricia, I wondered how to proceed.

"Feeling better?" I asked as I handed over the glass.

"Yes, thank you. Forgive me. I have behaved badly. It's just, well, it's just that Sheldon Junior never yells and we never argue. This was so unexpected, I kind of fell to pieces. I'm much better now."

I was startled at her abrupt change of demeanor. She shook her head like a boxer picking himself up off the mat and folded her hands in her lap.

"Good," I said, suspecting I had missed a golden opportunity to get her to blurt something significant. Oh, well. I'd just go back to plan A, whatever that was, and see if I could find out what part she had played in the case of the mysterious niece.

Here goes, I thought. "You may have heard that Fred Kroner donated some papers to the Historical Society before he died."

"I knew he was thinking about it. He asked me if I thought it was a good idea. I guess he was worried about revealing family secrets, but I assured him it was important to have the Kroners included in the Spencer County history. I'm glad to hear he followed through."

"Yes, he did, to the tune of six cartons."

"Anything interesting?"

"Mostly a jumble of odds and ends. There was a pamphlet from God's Fellowship. I guess you gave that to him." I wondered if she would own up to enticing him into the sect.

"Oh, no. He must have gotten that himself. Evidently he had been watching Johnny's Sunday night services on television and wrote away for it. I didn't even know he was interested in our Fellowship until he filled out the information sheet when he made a contribution and asked to have someone call on him."

I found that highly unlikely, but I tried to keep my face neutral, nodding ever so slightly.

"When was that?"

"A couple of months before he died. He knew his time was drawing to a close, and he was struggling to make peace with his God. I considered it a privilege to help him along the path toward salvation. Why all the questions, Jessie?"

"I came across some other material that needs explaining. Since you are so knowledgeable about genealogy, I thought you could clear up things for me. Where did Mr. Kroner get the idea that a long-lost niece named Johanna existed? In fact, what or who convinced him so completely that he made her the sole heir of his estate?"

I had Patricia's full attention now.

"It was you, wasn't it?"

"I don't know what you are talking about," she said.

"I think you do."

Patricia looked every which way except at me while her fingers were making confetti out of the wad of tissues in her lap. "You better leave now," she said.

"I think not. Not until you explain these documents I found in Mr. Kroner's papers," I said and pulled the envelope addressed to Fred Kroner in care of Patricia Fowler out of my purse. I emptied the contents onto the sofa next to her.

She snatched them up and started ripping them into shreds.

"Rip away," I said. "Those are copies. The originals are safely locked away."

"Why are you doing this to me?" The wailing started again.

"Oh, shut up," I said. "I'm doing this to you because you tried to take advantage of a lonely old man. God knows what would have happened if he hadn't died before you had your whole scam in place. 'Course he did kind of gum up the works when he made that new will. You probably thought you could introduce the phony Johanna Kroner to him and convince him to start handing over his money then and there."

I was definitely winging it, pulling suppositions out of my hat right and left. I had no idea if any of them were true. Patricia sat there, staring at me, her mouth wide open.

"Well, what do you have to say for yourself? I called Walnut Creek and they told me that no Thomas Kroner had ever lived there. They figured you had confused Kroner with the Kromer family. When they informed you of that, you asked them to send you the Kromer information. You were going to 'use it in a workshop to illustrate pitfalls in genealogical research.' Instead, you altered the documents to convince Mr. Kroner that Johanna did exist."

Patricia sat up straight and carefully folded her hands in her lap. "Jessie, you are making some very serious accusations. Do you think you can listen to the truth instead of accusing me of being a scam artist?"

I nodded. It was my turn to sit quietly.

"You're right. Fred Kroner was a lonely old man. He never married and his only family was two brothers he hadn't spoken to for forty years and a nephew who called once a month to see if he was still alive. Even though he had found God, there was still a hole in his life. When I mentioned that I was pretty sure there had been a Kroner family in Walnut Creek, he asked me to investigate and see if maybe they were related."

"Why didn't you tell him the truth when you found out you were wrong?"

"His hopes were so high, I knew it would break his heart, so I altered the documents and let him believe in Johanna. I knew he didn't have long to live. He'd told me what the doctors had said. I like to believe what I did falls under the heading of Christian charity."

CHAPTER 23

"Christian charity?" It was all I could do to keep from scream-ing at her. "Christian charity? Are you out of your mind? That was one of the most deceitful, dishonest, immoral things I have ever heard."

Patricia started weeping into her sodden tissues again, but I could have cared less.

"And whose bright idea was it to create a phony Johanna and then have her bumped off before she could reveal the plan? Was it your equally phony Reverend Johnny? And where did Floyd fit into all of this? Did he figure out what was going on and threaten to expose you and the reverend, so he had to be disposed of too?"

I guess I went too far. When I get angry, my mouth often rushes ahead of my brain. Patricia jumped up, grabbed my arm, yanked me to my feet, and pushed me toward the door. "Get out of here."

She pulled open the door and pushed me out. Only a quick lunge for the banister kept me from tumbling down the staircase. I sat down on the top step to catch my breath and review my disastrous confrontation with Patricia. I was amazed that Sheldon Senior had not heard the ruckus and come to investigate. Then it occurred to me the sound proofing between the residential area and the first-floor parlors would have to be extraordinary so that the patrons' families and friends, and the patrons themselves, would not be disturbed (now that was a ghoulish thought).

As I continued to sit there on the top step, I didn't like to admit it, but Patricia may have been telling the truth when she said she thought her deception was an act of Christian charity. I wondered what she and Sheldon had been fighting about. My guess was his relationship with the reverend. What was it she had said? Oh yes, "before I could pretend." I had never known Sheldon to get emotional or raise his voice, even as a kid. However, as Aunt Henrietta would say, "Still waters run deep."

I pulled myself up by the same banister that had saved me from a fall and headed to the first floor. The chime sounded softly again as I let myself out the door and escaped back into the real world.

What a mess, I thought. What if Patricia's only sin was spinning a tale to make a lonely old man feel better, how did that figure into the arson and the murder of Ruby Holliday? Who had ordered that? And who was the man with a sling and Cubs baseball cap who had been with Floyd? That reminded me. I needed to call Gil and see what they found out from the autopsy. I was close to the courthouse, so I decided to stop by.

Gil was actually in his office.

"Want to have dinner tonight?" I asked. "Make up for the lousy company I was last night." I had decided to wait and tell him about the genealogy scam Patricia had pulled. Maybe he'd tell me if he had any results from the autopsy on Floyd.

"Sounds good," he said. "I'll be finished up here by six. Where do you want to go?"

"How about Chez Jessie?"

"Great. I'll bring the wine."

"No need. There are several bottles left from the weekend."

"I've got good news for you," Gil said. "Want to hear it now or wait till this evening?" He grinned, knowing full well that waiting was not my style.

"Please feel free to tell me right this minute."

"I know who locked you in the storeroom."

"Oh, my God. That didn't take long. Who?"

"First of all, it was not some malignant plot. It was accidental."

"Wait a minute. How could it have been an accident? I was yelling and pounding on the door. You'd have to be deaf as a stone not to hear me."

"That's exactly the case. Wilbur, the night custodian, is deaf as a stone. He saw the basement lights on and went downstairs to check things out. He saw the key in the outside lock, figured someone had forgotten to return it, so he locked the door, went back upstairs, turned out the lights, replaced the key in Virginia's drawer, and proceeded to finish his work for the evening."

"You've got to be kidding."

"Nope. Virginia's the one who figured it out. When Wilbur came in this afternoon, he works from two to ten, Virginia asked him if he'd seen anything or anybody unusual last night. He told her the only thing out of the ordinary was that someone had left the basement lights on and the Historical Society storeroom key had been left in the lock."

"Wait a minute," I said. "If he's so deaf he couldn't hear me, how could Virginia talk to him?"

"He's a great lip reader. He was really upset when he found out what he'd done and asked me to apologize to you. He even offered to quit. I, of course, said no. So anyway, mystery solved. No one was trying to do you bodily harm. It was a simple accident."

"Well, it didn't feel so simple to me, and I hope you stressed to Wilbur that next time he check to make sure no one is in the room." I didn't say so, but I was almost disappointed that's all it was. I'd convinced myself that it was part of an effort to scare me off. Of course, scare me off what I hadn't yet determined.

"I'll see you a little after six," I said.

I had to make a stop at the supermarket before I headed home. As usual, my refrigerator was approaching empty.

The message light was blinking on the telephone. I decided to put my groceries away and get dinner started before I checked who had called. No hurry, because it was sure to be either Henrietta or Frank with their daily check-in.

I seasoned the chicken and popped it into the oven to roast. I'd supplement it with pilaf out-of-a-box, tossed salad, and rolls from the freezer section I would finish off in the oven right before we ate. The good thing about roasting a chicken was there should be enough left so I wouldn't need to cook for a couple of days. Besides it tastes good. I'd let Gil do the carving.

I tidied up the kitchen and put clean placemats and napkins on the table. Too bad it was November. I couldn't run out to the garden and cut some flowers to brighten things up. The flowers in the supermarket had looked as dreary as the sky outdoors, so I settled for a colorful pottery figure.

I punched the play button on the answering machine, but instead of Frank or Henrietta, it was the sonorous tones of Reverend Smythe that greeted my ear.

"Miss Schroeder, this is John Smythe. Patsy told me you found my address book. I'll be in Riverport tomorrow to consult with Floyd's family about his service. I will call and make arrangements to pick it up. Looking forward to seeing you again."

Oh, great. Just what I wanted. Another visit with the good reverend. At least I could ask him why my name was in his little black book.

I looked at the clock. I just had time to shower and change before Gil arrived. I was feeling guilty, because it had been several days since had I taken a run. Tomorrow, I promised myself. I'd even make myself take the seven-mile loop to make up for my laziness.

The phone was ringing as I stepped out of the shower. "Great. What now?" I muttered as I wrapped a towel around myself.

"Just wanted to tell you, I'll be a little late," Gil said.

A little late? What else was new?

"What now?" I asked, a little more curtly than I should have.

"Right after you left, Floyd's dad and uncle showed up, and I just now got them out of the office. What a pair. I can see why Fred hadn't talked to his brothers for forty years. I have about thirty minutes of paperwork to finish up and then I'll be directly over. I'll tell you about the visit when I get there."

"No problem," I said. "See you about seven." That was an interesting development.

After I turned down the oven, I washed the salad greens and put the salad together. It was ready to be tossed. I also cooked the pilaf. I could reheat it in the microwave when we were ready to eat. Thank heavens for microwaves. Gil sounded like he was in a talkative mood. I didn't want anything that might distract him.

I pondered the pros and cons of telling him about my discovery of the altered genealogy records and my confrontation with Patricia. I thought he would be interested in the former, but a bit put out with me over the latter. I'd make my decision after I gauged his mood.

A few minutes past seven his patrol car pulled into the drive. I had the door open, waiting for him as he came up the walk. He enveloped me in a hug even before he took off his coat.

"Um, you smell good," he said. "Or is that dinner?"

"Both. Here give me your coat. I expect you need a drink after coping with the Kroner brothers."

"That is a fact, but I think I'll just have a glass of wine. I may have to go back to the office."

I poured him a glass of red. Even though we were having

chicken, I had discovered that Gil was not a fan of white wine, so I'd opened a nice pinot noir.

"Let's sit in the living room," I said. "I finally got the fireplace cleaned out after the reverend's fiasco. What a mess. So what's up with the Kroner boys?" I asked after we got settled.

"They want me to arrest your reverend. They are convinced he murdered Floyd."

"Now that's interesting. What gave them that idea?"

"As best as I could figure out, they called the lawyer to ask when they would get their share of the money since they are Floyd's only living relatives. The lawyer explained the provision that gave the money to Reverend Smythe if Floyd died before his uncle or before the will was probated."

"What a family! The first thing they think of after their only son and nephew dies is how much money they will come into. What'd you tell them?"

"I explained that there was no evidence of foul play. That Floyd had died as the result of massive head injuries."

"Is that what the autopsy concluded?" I asked.

"That's the preliminary report. We have to wait till the tox results come back before they issue the final."

"And did that satisfy the brothers?"

"It did not. It only incensed them further. After much ranting and raving, they stomped out, muttering that they would take care of that phony minister themselves since the law wouldn't help them. If I were Reverend Smythe, I'd steer clear of the brothers."

"That may be difficult," I said. "He's planning to be in Riverport tomorrow to consult with the brothers about Floyd's funeral service."

"How did you find that out?"

"He called. He left something here the night of the ice storm and wants to pick it up. Do you have a problem with that?"

Gil sighed. "No, I don't have a problem with that. It's just that slick televangelists bother me. They don't get to be successful unless they can worm their way into people's confidence."

"Don't worry. My cynical antenna is fully extended."

"I know. Tell him to call me. I need to talk to him about how to handle the boys. He should stay away from them and let Sheldon take care of the arrangements, at least until they settle down."

It always amused me to hear the Kroner brothers referred to as "the boys." They were both well into their seventies.

"I'll pass the information along to the reverend."

"No, Jessie, you stay out of it. I'll take care of it."

He was using that authoritative tone of voice I couldn't stand, but I chose to keep my mouth shut.

I decided not to tell Gil about the various happenings, particularly I didn't mention that I was in the reverend's little black book. The information about Patricia's phony genealogy of Johanna Kroner could wait. He already knew the body was a plant.

It turned out to be a lovely low-key evening. Even the chicken was good, though a little dry. Gil seemed to be impressed. It was too early in our relationship for me to confess that it was one of only three main dishes that I could produce. He left a little after ten. We had decided that discretion was the best course of action for now.

CHAPTER 24

The sun was making a valiant effort to shine, but the jury was still out on which was going to win, the sun or the November gloom.

I decided to delay my run until I heard from the reverend. My computer was taunting me from the corner, so I went over and switched it on. I'd work on *You Can't Judge a Book by Its Cover.* It was time for some serious writing. I'd made notes of Betsy and Joey's comments and questions and needed to figure out how to incorporate them. It would be a nice story, not as quirky as *Ghosts,* but good. I especially liked the scene with Timmy and the cat on the tree branch peering through the leaves. That would make a great illustration.

I had been at work for an hour when the telephone rang. I hit save and went to answer.

"Miss Schroeder, good morning. It's John Smythe."

"Good morning, Reverend. How are you?"

"Oh, dear. I thought you were going to call me John."

"Sorry, John." I guess he thought his manner was beguiling. Well, I could play that game too. "And how about dropping the Miss Schroeder and calling me Jessie?"

"Sounds good. I've got a pretty full day in Riverport. If it's all right with you, I will send my driver, William, to pick up the address book."

Driver? I didn't know he had a driver. He had been alone the night of the ice storm.

"I didn't realize you used a driver, John. Weren't you by yourself the night you came to my door?"

"I was. When I combine business with pleasure, I drive myself. I knew I was going to spend an extra day with Patsy and Sheldon. When I'm strictly on church business I have William drive. It's amazing how much work you can get done while you're on the road. I dare say at least half of my sermons are composed in the back seat of my car."

"What time will he be by?" I asked. "I need to get my run in before it gets too late."

"That's right. I remember Floyd, bless his soul, mentioned that you were a big runner. Hold on a minute."

I heard him talking to someone, but I couldn't make out the words.

"How about two o'clock?"

"That's fine. I'll be back by then. By the way, I have a message for you from the Sheriff." I started to tell him to call Gil, but decided I was perfectly capable of passing along the message myself. "He thinks it's not a good idea for you to go see the Kroner brothers. He recommends you let Sheldon handle the discussions with them."

"Really? Why?"

"You probably should talk to the Sheriff."

"I'll do that, but give me a clue as to what's going on."

"Well, they've gotten the idea that you somehow were responsible for Floyd's death." I softened the accusation Gil had reported to me.

I've heard people use the term pregnant pause, and that was an apt description for the silence on the other end of the phone.

"Did I hear you correctly?" he finally said. "They think I caused Floyd's death? Where did that idea come from?"

"I'm not sure," I said. "Something to do with the will, I think. You really should talk to the Sheriff."

"Fine. I'll do that. William will be by at two for the address book."

He ended the conversation, but before the connection was broken I heard him say, "We've got . . ." And then silence.

I replaced my own receiver and walked over to the window. *We've got what? And who is "we"?*

I pondered those two questions all the way around my seven-mile loop and was no closer to answers at the end than I was at the beginning.

It seemed like half of Spencer County was out on the road. Most of them just honked and waved as they went by, but several, as usual, stopped to see if I didn't need a ride. It never ceased to amaze me why someone would think I wanted a ride, dressed as I was in my running outfit and shoes and pounding the blacktop.

Frank went zooming by in his pickup, then screeched to a halt when he saw it was me, and waited for me to catch up with him.

"Hey, Cuz, how's it going?"

"It's going just fine, but I'll probably freeze to death if I have to stand here," I said, running in place.

"Wanted you to know the kids keep talking about your new story. They really liked it. Joey can't wait for spring. He wants to start climbing trees."

"Tell him after it warms up. Now I gotta go."

The sun came out just as I turned back into my drive. I stopped for a minute to look at my home. It was a classic two-story, white-frame farmhouse. A little cupola, perched on the roof, gave it a whimsical air. I noticed several patches of peeling paint. Next spring I needed to get the paint crew out. It was easier to think about home maintenance than the mayhem that seemed to abound around me.

After my shower and lunch, I tried to do more work on my

story, but the muse had abandoned me. Instead, I checked my E-mail and answered several.

A few minutes before two o'clock, I heard a car and, as I reached the window, a big black sedan with tinted windows was pulling up to the gate. Apparently, preachers had the same car code as funeral directors. As I watched, the driver, wearing a black leather jacket and black slacks, got out. He had on some kind of a cap. He stopped and looked around, making a full 360-degree survey of the house and yard. I wondered if he were killing time or getting the lay of the land. Finally, he opened the gate and came up to the door. I let him wait a minute before I answered his knock.

When I opened the door, I found myself staring at a man who looked to be a little older than me. He was short and slender and probably would be described as wiry. He kept his hands in his pockets as if to assure me that he meant me no harm. But what rendered me speechless for a minute was what he had on his head—a Chicago Cubs baseball cap.

"I'm William," he said. "I'm here to get Reverend Smythe's address book."

Without thinking, I blurted out, "Where's your sling?"

"I beg your pardon."

"Your sling. Weren't you wearing a sling the night you went drinking with Floyd, the night of the ice storm?"

He didn't miss a beat. "I don't know what you're talking about, ma'am. You must have me mixed up with someone else. Now the address book, please."

I picked up the book from the countertop and handed it to him.

"Thank you, ma'am," he said as he tipped his cap and headed back toward the car.

I closed the door and put on the dead bolt before I walked over to the window. He had paused at the gate. He pulled a cell phone out of his jacket pocket and punched in a number. He turned back and stared at the house. I'm sure he knew I was watching him. He finally went out through the gate, talking on the phone as he went. I stood there until the car pulled onto the blacktop and accelerated up the hill toward Frank and Mildred's house.

I had been holding my breath. I took a big gulp of air and walked over to the phone and called the nonemergency number for the Sheriff's office.

Virginia, as usual, answered before the second ring.

"It's Jessie Schroeder. Is the Sheriff there?"

"Oh, hi there, Ms. Schroeder. Sorry, he and Clarence are on a call. Some kind of backup for the state police out on the Interstate. I think it's a drug bust. Those drug dealers seem to think the Interstates were built exclusively for them to move their stuff. At least once a week we get called on to help. Is there something I can do for you?"

Figures, I thought. *Seems like Gil is never around when I need him.*

"No, Virginia, just have him call me at his earliest convenience."

I hung up the phone and paced back and forth in the kitchen. William was genuinely creepy, and I'd bet the farm that he was the one who had been with Floyd. The fact he worked for Reverend Smythe was a nail in the reverend's coffin, as far as I was concerned.

God, where did that come from—bet the farm and nail in the coffin? I had definitely been spending too much time around Henrietta.

I finally stopped my pacing and sat down at the table and tried to recreate the sequence of events surrounding Fred Kroner, his death, and the will.

Patricia had befriended him, in hopes, I assumed, of bringing him and his money into God's Fellowship. Somewhere along the way, she convinced him he had a long-lost niece. Now, the $64,000 question: Did she do it on purpose from the beginning or did she think it was a possibility and only later discovered she was mistaken? And why bother? My gut feeling was that Patricia had not done it on purpose, but I had no proof either way.

Then where did Johanna Kroner, aka Ruby Holliday, come from? Obviously someone had hired her, but when and why and why had she been killed? Had Patricia told the reverend that there was no real niece and then he or one of his people had brought in Ruby in hopes of running an old-fashioned scam on Mr. Kroner? But their plans were thwarted because the Grim Reaper had come calling before the scam could produce results, ergo, Ruby was dispensable.

And why get rid of Floyd? I leaned back for a few minutes and reviewed what I knew about Floyd. He had been an unpleasant little man. As a kid he had been greedy and sneaky, always spying on the other kids. He would have made it his business to know exactly what was going on. Maybe he tried a little blackmail in hopes of getting more, maybe even all, of his uncle's money. Is that what he and Patricia had been talking about in the parking lot? I didn't think so. Patricia had indicated it was about her husband. Had William slipped something into Floyd's drink before he put him in his car and pointed it downhill?

The more I tried to put things together, the more I became convinced that I was missing an important element. But what? Maybe a shot of caffeine would straighten out the muddle. But before I could get my coffee, the telephone rang. Gil!

"Jessie, this is Sheldon Junior. How are you?"

Sheldon Junior. Was he going to berate me for upsetting his wife?

"I'm just fine, thank you. And yourself?"

"Excellent. I hope I'm not disturbing you, but I just had to call and say thank you."

Thank you? What was this about?

"My dear Jessie, if it hadn't been for you, we might have had another disaster on our hands," Sheldon Junior continued. "Thank heavens you warned the reverend about the Kroner boys. I convinced him to wait in the car while I talked to them first. They had the bizarre notion that John had done something to cause Floyd's death. It took some doing, but I finally calmed them down, and they agreed they were wrong."

I had never heard him string so many words together before.

He let out a big sigh. "I shudder to think what would have happened if John had walked into their house. They had a shotgun right by the front door. Knowing them, they would have shot first and asked questions later. Anyway, John wants to say something."

"Jessie, my dear, I must thank you. You may have saved my life for a second time. And Shelly was marvelous. I told him he should apply to the diplomatic corp. I don't know how he did it, but he had those two old goats eating out of his hand. Again, my heartfelt thanks."

Interesting, I thought, but what I really wanted was to talk to Gil.

He finally called back. I could not have scripted a more unsatisfactory conversation if I tried. When I told him about William and his Chicago Cubs cap, he said, "Jessie, do you have any idea how many thousands of men from the Chicago area own and wear a Cubs cap? Did you hear what I said? I said thousands."

It was not like Gil to be so sarcastic. I started in on my litany of why he should take this seriously, but he did not let me get past reason number two before he interrupted.

"Look, Jessie, I'm sorry. You may be right. I'll check into it, but please let it go for now."

His voice sounded funny. "Is something wrong?" I asked.

"I'll be gone for the next couple of days. I have to go to Chicago. I just found out an hour ago my friend Greg, you know the one who owns the cabin . . ."

I heard him take a deep breath.

"I just found out he was shot and killed two days ago, trying to break up a robbery. He wasn't even on duty when it happened."

"Oh, Gil, I am so sorry. Is there anything I can do? Why don't you come over for a while? Or I can come to you." His voice had sounded so sad, it broke my heart.

"It wasn't till they were making out the list of pall bearers that they realized they had forgotten to call me. Oh, Jessie, he was such a good man and a good cop."

"I'm sorry I didn't get to meet him."

"I told him all about you. He said you sounded too good for me. We were even talking about getting together so I could introduce you."

"When are you leaving?" I asked.

"As soon as I straighten things out in the office. I have to bring Clarence up to speed and alert the State Police that I will be gone."

"Drive carefully and call me from Chicago."

"I'll try, but I can't promise. I'll be back Saturday. You know I love you."

CHAPTER 25

I spent a restless night. I finally gave up trying to sleep and got out of bed, even though it wasn't light yet. Genevieve was still curled up on her favorite chair when I staggered into the kitchen. By the time I sat down with my first cup of coffee, the sky was starting to lighten. Gil would have made it to Chicago. It was about a five-hour drive from Riverport. The service for his friend was scheduled for tomorrow, Friday.

As I worked on my second cup, I started to remember scraps of the dreams that had roiled my night's sleep. One in particular stood out vividly. Reverend Smythe and Sheldon were standing in front of a door. First the reverend bowed and said, "After you, my dear Shelly." Then Sheldon bowed and said, "No, no, after you, my dear John." They kept repeating the routine until I had gotten bored and moved on to another dream.

I couldn't help but compare the "after you, dear" dream with my general impression of the two men and what I knew of their relationship. They were almost bubbly in their camaraderie during the phone conversation, calling each other John and Shelly. When I thought about it, I had never heard anyone call Sheldon "Shelly" before.

The judge had scheduled one of the special meetings of the Library Board for one o'clock today. Budget problems—libraries never had enough money. Come hell or high water—another Henrietta-ism—I was going to find a way to have a private talk with Sheldon.

Mildred called a little after ten. She wanted to discuss Thanksgiving dinner. I had lost track of time and had forgotten it was in a week. Mildred and Frank, as usual, would host, and, also as usual, I knew I should start dieting immediately. Mildred put on a spread that would have made the Pilgrims proud.

"Jessie, dear, could I ask you a huge favor?" Mildred said.

"No problem. What do you need?"

"Do you think you can find the recipe for your mother's cranberry-orange relish? It is the perfect foil for the bourbon, brown-sugar sweet potatoes and the cheesy creamed onions."

I almost groaned thinking about the meal. Most people, when they made creamed onions, bought the little bags of frozen pearl onions, blanched and peeled and ready to go. Others bought the whole dish, already prepared and frozen. Not Mildred. She started with baskets of pearl onions. She blanched and peeled them one by one, carefully trimming the root ends so the onions didn't disintegrate as they simmered in the sauce that was so good it defied description. And the sweet potatoes! She always turned a deaf ear to Frank's plea not to use his good JD. "This is no time to be a cheapskate," she would tell him as she poured in a generous measure.

"I'll dig it out," I said. "How much do you want me to make?"

"Oh, no, you are much too busy. Frank'll come by this afternoon to pick it up."

Smart woman. She knew if I attempted to make the relish, something would go wrong. We made arrangements for me to leave the recipe in the kitchen door, since I would be at the library.

I spent the rest of the morning going through Mom's recipes. It was a wonderful diversion to the mess around me. She kept a notebook with pockets that were stuffed full of recipes cut out of newspapers and magazines. The most fun were the note cards in her handwriting of recipes she had copied from friends, many with cryptic notes, such as, "Susan always uses way too much sugar," with "way" underlined.

I found the relish recipe on a yellowed card covered with brown splotches. The handwriting was not immediately recognizable. Then I realized it was my grandmother's. I looked at the card almost reverently. What a wonderful legacy. From mother to daughter and now to granddaughter. I got a new three by five card out and copied the recipe for Mildred. No way was I going to let the original leave my house.

By the time I arrived at the library the rest of the group was gathered and ready to go. Everybody was in attendance. Sheldon wore his usual suit, tie, and white shirt. No pastels or even creams for him. I took the seat beside him. The rest of us were decidedly more casual. Even the judge was in corduroys with a sweater over his open-necked shirt.

The question before us was whether we should recommend to the County Commissioners and Town Council that they put an eighth of a cent increase in the sales tax before the voters, the money to be dedicated to the library.

Actually the question was not whether to recommend the tax increase—that had been quickly settled with a 7 to 0 yes vote—but how best to sell it to the voters. The discussion was lively with everyone participating, except Sheldon who sat quietly. No sign of the bubbly conversationalist I had talked with yesterday. By three o'clock a plan of action was set, and the judge and I were elected to make the presentation to a joint City-County meeting.

As Sheldon gathered his papers to leave, I leaned over. "I need to talk to you," I said. "Could you stay a few minutes?"

He looked startled then glanced at his watch as if to indicate he had vital matters to attend to.

"It's really important," I said. "It won't take long."

"Patricia's expecting me home," he said.

"It won't take long," I repeated.

We waited until the others had filed out of the room, then he turned to me. "What is it?"

I went through my confrontation with Patricia step by step. "I don't know why she decided to lie to Mr. Kroner. She claims it was out of Christian charity, but I find that to be a spurious explanation. I think it has something to do with her relationship with Reverend Smythe and her desire to bring money into God's Fellowship, and specifically to the reverend."

All the time I was talking to Sheldon, I watched him closely. I could not discern a single change of expression or twitch and except for an occasional blink, not a flicker of his eyes. "What do you think?" I asked.

He turned slightly away from me and looked over my shoulder, "I don't know. What does the Sheriff say?"

"I haven't had a chance to tell him yet. He had to go to Chicago for the funeral of a friend. He does know the identification of the body, and it definitely is not Johanna Kroner."

"Are you going to tell the Sheriff?"

"Of course, as soon as he gets back."

"I see," he said and set about gathering up his papers.

"What about the reverend?"

"What about him?"

"I guess you're pretty close."

"Whatever gave you that idea?" He made a great show of tidying up his stack of papers, moving them ever so slightly this way and that until the margins were even.

Something is screwy here, I thought and just shrugged. "Thanks for your time, and tell Patricia I'm sorry if I upset her. She's the one who should tell the Sheriff, not me."

Sheldon nodded and quickly left the boardroom, carrying his coat over his arm. He didn't want to chance anymore time alone with me, not even the time it took to put his overcoat on.

Wilma was standing at the circulation desk talking to the librarian when I came out. "Wait up, Jessie," she called. "I'll walk to the car with you."

As she got in step with me, she said, "What was that all about?"

"Nothing special," I said, deciding to keep my suspicions to myself for the time being. "Just some information for Patricia."

Wilma crinkled her nose. "She's a queer duck, if you ask me. She's supposed to be this expert in genealogy, but she's always jumping to conclusions, and I find her to be pretty sloppy in her research. Maybe she's inhaled too many fumes from the embalming fluid."

I had to laugh. "Wilma, that's terrible. I think it's the fumes from the bourbon bottle that are the problem. Besides, that's something I'd say, not you."

Wilma entwined her arm in mine. "Who's to say who's the teacher and who's the student?"

Over my meager dinner that night, if dinner it could be called, I tried to make sense out of my conversation with Sheldon. Damn, I had meant to ask him what he knew about the reverend's driver, William. I needed to start writing things down.

According to the *Spencer County Argus* that had arrived this morning, visitation for Floyd was set for tomorrow at the Fowler Funeral Home and the service on Saturday at the Abundant Life Church with the Reverend John W. Smythe, Jr., officiating. Floyd would be laid to rest in the family plot along with his Uncle Fred. Somehow, though I wasn't sure how yet, that seemed fitting.

After dinner, I tried reading, but could not keep my mind on the storyline. Then I turned on the television, but the *Law and Order* rerun, even though it was one I hadn't seen before, could not hold my attention. I'd never asked Gil if he liked *Law and Order* and its multiple spin-offs. The original was my favorite. I wondered how things were going with Gil. He sounded so sad. Maybe if I went out to the kitchen, he would call.

The phone did ring as soon as I walked into the kitchen, but it was Cousin Frank, not Gil.

"How's it going, Cuz?" he asked, using his favorite salutation.

"Fine. Are you going to Floyd's visitation tomorrow?"

"Probably. Want a ride?"

"Sure. It goes from six to eight."

"How about if I pick you up a little before six? That way we can get there, sign the book, and leave before the rest of Riverport and Spencer County arrives."

"Sounds good. See you tomorrow."

I had no sooner hung up than the phone rang again. This time it was Gil.

"Hi, hon," he said.

"Hi, yourself. How are you doing?"

"Pretty good. I'm on my way to the wake. Figured I'd better check in while I still could. The old gang all showed up, and I'm sure it'll go pretty late. Greg's son and daughter are here, and we had a good visit. I hadn't seen them since they were little. Even his ex is supposed to arrive tomorrow. Just talked to Clarence. He says all is quiet on the home front. What's up with you?"

"Not much." I decided to spare him my speculations. There would be plenty of time for that when he got back home. "The Library Board decided to recommend a tax increase. If the powers that be agree, I'll be pretty busy campaigning. It will probably be on the ballot in March. When will you be home?"

"Hopefully in time for dinner Saturday. Interested?"

"Absolutely, but promise me one thing."

"What's that?"

"Make sure someone else drives tonight. I want you home in one piece."

"Not a problem. Miss you."

"Miss you, too."

No sooner had I replaced the receiver than it rang again. *What now?* I thought, as I said hello.

"Why are you doing this? Leave us alone." No preamble, no identification.

The words were slurred. I could almost smell the alcohol. I was sure it was Patricia, but before I could respond, the receiver on the other end was slammed down.

This whole thing was getting too much for me. I was beginning to suspect that there was something in the municipal drinking water that made everyone a little loopy. Whoever said small-town living was quiet and uncomplicated obviously had never lived in one, especially Riverport.

Hopefully tomorrow would be uneventful, so I could work on *You Can't Judge a Book by Its Cover* and then take a long run before I went to Floyd's visitation with Frank.

CHAPTER 26

For the first time in at least a week, the sun was shining brightly when I awoke. Maybe that was a good omen for the day.

By nine o'clock I was hard at work at my computer. My spell-check kept alerting me to mistakes. I'm not a bad speller. I've met a few worse. It's just that my typing skills are abominable. After a quick break for lunch, I returned to work. At the stroke of three, I leaned back and read the two pages I had finished.

"I think it's going to be good," I said to Genevieve who seemed to think it was her duty to sleep on my desk next to the keyboard in case I felt a sudden urge to give her a scratch. She gave me a bored look and opened her mouth in a huge yawn. "I can see you are impressed," I said as I gave her the rub she had been waiting for.

I stood and rolled my shoulders to unkink my muscles. A run was definitely what I needed. I had enough time for the five-mile route before dusk, then a quick shower and I'd be ready when Frank got here a little before six.

The sun was still shining, and the temperature had moderated from last week's arctic blast. The icy patches along the road had turned into puddles and now were waiting for the sun to set so they could freeze again. I knew I'd work up a good sweat by the time I got to the top of the hill just beyond Frank and Mildred's place.

As I settled into my pace, my mind began to regurgitate the information I knew or had postulated about the mystery surrounding Fred Kroner's will and the phantom niece. I had been so distracted by my developing relationship with Gil and the demands of my new Emily story that I had done nothing more than leave any clues in a jumble in the back of my mind. Now was the time to sort them out.

I debated how to do that for a minute as I ran in place, letting a car go by before I moved to the other side of the road. Another black sedan with tinted windows. They must have been running a special on them at the car dealership.

I wrote stories and stories used plots. I had a notion what the impetus behind the whole affair was—that good old-fashioned standby, greed. I would take what I knew and use it to create a plot and see if it fit.

It had all started when Patricia Fowler befriended Mr. Kroner in her search for converts to and monetary support for God's Fellowship Church. The founder of the church was her long-time friend John W. Smythe, Jr., who had been raised by her family. The reverend had introduced Patricia to Sheldon. Evidentially Sheldon and the reverend had a longtime relationship, and Sheldon served on the board of God's Fellowship Foundation.

The next part was a bit murky. Patricia convinced Mr. Kroner she had discovered a long-lost niece of his. Did she deliberately mislead him or was it a mistake on her part? It hardly mattered which it was, but for the sake of the story, I decided she'd misled him and was going to produce the false niece who would bilk Mr. Kroner out of large sums of money. I assumed the fictitious niece would receive a cut of the monies, with the bulk going to Reverend Smythe.

Old Mr. Kroner screwed up the whole plan by making a new will leaving his money to the niece and then promptly dying. Of course, there was no niece, and the phony one, Ruby Holliday, probably had demanded big money to keep quiet about the intended scam, so Ruby was disposed of.

The secondary legatees were nephew Floyd Kroner and Reverend Smythe. Floyd somehow had found out about the scam and the phony niece and threatened to expose the reverend and his church unless he also received a cut from the reverend's share, so he was disposed of.

I made my turn to start the homeward leg of the run. The whole thing was pretty broad brush and I assumed that Patricia and Reverend Smythe were the prime movers. I had trouble with that assumption. I didn't think the reverend would do something that obvious. I supposed it could have all been Patricia's idea, but I didn't think she was that clever. And where did Sheldon fit in? Then there was the reverend's driver, William, with his Cubs baseball cap. Was he the enforcer? If so, who had hired him? Enough of that for now! I was almost home.

I could see the flag was down on my mailbox as I jogged down the hill. I crossed the road to collect my mail, even though I knew it would be mostly bills and catalogs. Right on top was a postcard from my friend Diana who had gone to London for a week of theater. As I stood by the mailbox, trying to decipher her tiny printing in the fading light, I heard a noise. I looked up just in time to see a big black fender heading straight toward me.

I threw myself backward into the bramble, but not quickly enough. The metal brushed my side and I went flying, landing with a crash in a scrub cedar some feet behind the mailbox. Mail fluttered around me. I heard a screech of brakes and a car backing up. A whoosh sounded as an automatic window lowered, and I could just make out voices.

"Did we get her?"

"Yeah, I think so, but I better check."

I heaved myself up. My left ankle hurt like hell but I'd worry about that later. I headed straight back into the woods.

"There she goes," a man yelled.

"Shoot the bitch!" yelled another man as I scrambled behind a large oak tree, pivoted, and hopped and lurched into the gathering darkness.

I could have sworn one of the voices sounded familiar, but like my ankle, I'd think about that later, because I heard and felt the whine of a bullet as it passed by my shoulder.

I picked up as much speed as I could. I was on the path that led down to McGee Creek. There were pounding footsteps behind me and I could only hope whoever was pursuing me would trip on one of the roots that snaked across the trail. Once I got to the creek, I would have to make a decision. Leave the path and crawl into one of the undercuts in the bank of the creek, or cross the water.

My ankle was throbbing so badly, the idea of stopping was becoming more imperative. Only one problem: The undercuts were favorite nesting and hibernation spots for the copperheads that frequented the stream banks. But if I forded the creek, I had to make my way across a small clearing before I'd find safety in the trees. I tripped and fell on my injured ankle, making the decision for me. It was all I could do to keep from screaming. I clenched my teeth and crawled off the path into the underbrush as far as I could and curled into a tight ball.

The footsteps behind me had slowed and there was much stumbling and cursing. Suddenly, the footsteps stopped and I could hear ragged breathing no more than a few feet from my hiding place.

Then, "Come on back, William. We gotta get out of here. Someone's going to see the car."

The same familiar voice.

"Move the goddamned car, Junior, but first bring me the flashlight from the glove box," William yelled back. "I'm gonna find the bitch if it takes all night."

Junior! I knew two Juniors. The reverend and Sheldon. And one of them was trying to kill me. Which one?

The footsteps moved away. I assumed William was going back to meet up with Junior and the flashlight.

I hoisted myself up on my hands and knees and worked my way farther from the path, moving in a diagonal toward the creek. Copperheads be damned! If I could make it, I was going into the first hidey hole I found in the bank.

I was almost there when I saw a flash of light coming my way. I flattened myself next to a pile of oak mold and with my hands frantically dug at the soft mold. If I could dig deep enough, maybe I'd have a hole to hide in. The light was coming closer and my heart sank as I saw I hadn't gotten as far off the path as I thought. I could hear the two men arguing.

"But William, where should I go? I can't just leave you here."

"Dammit, Junior, use your head. Go up the road a bit. There's a pullout where you can park. If someone comes along, just tell 'em you're using your cell phone. I'll leave mine on, so call if anything suspicious happens, then come back and get me."

"It's dark. I need the flashlight to find my way back."

"Jesus H. Christ!" William exploded. "The bitch will have made it to Timbuktu by the time I start looking for her."

"I doubt it," Junior said. "There was a lot of blood back there on the path. I think she's crawled off someplace. She won't be hard to find."

Then I had it. The unemotional monotone could belong to only one person. Junior was Sheldon Fowler, Jr.—fellow Library Board member, Patricia's husband, and Riverport's mortician.

The light moved back up the path. I guessed Sheldon had won the argument. At least now I knew which way to head. As I crawled deeper into the woods, I heard a car engine start and saw the light moving back down the path, sweeping back and forth. I had managed to put a good distance between William and me.

I hadn't realized I was bleeding, but when I felt around my ankle, my sock was sticky with blood. It seemed to have congealed, so maybe I wasn't leaving a trail behind me anymore. Not much I could do if I was.

The next thing I knew I was falling, and then darkness.

When I came to, it was pitch black, and I was wet and freezing. I had found the creek. I must have hit my head when I went tumbling over the edge. Fortunately the water level was low, but my feet and legs were soaked, and the rocks jabbed into my behind. Hypothermia was all I could think of as I hitched my way to a sitting position and pulled myself out of the water and partway up the bank. I grabbed hold of a tree root sticking out of the bank, so I wouldn't slip back down. I didn't know if I had enough strength to make it to the top.

I could hear a siren in the distance. Did that mean someone was coming to save me? Was Gil back from Chicago? I reached up and felt my head. There was a knot on the back and my hair was a mat of mud and dead leaves. My eyes were slowly adjusting to the dark. This time of year, the canopy of branches overhead was leafless. I touched my ankle, wincing at the light touch. At least the cold water had numbed it a bit. It had swelled to the circumference of a grapefruit.

I couldn't just sit here. Hypothermia would become a reality. I was afraid to start yelling. As far as I knew, William was still combing the woods in his quest to "finish off the bitch."

"No one's going to save you but yourself, so get going, Jessie," I muttered to myself.

I reached behind me with my free hand, feeling for another tree root as I pushed myself up with my good leg. I tried to remember the height of the bank—at least ten feet on this side. A pale moon cast a faint shimmer of light on the water and rocks below me.

It felt like it took hours, but finally I reached the lip of the bank. With one final heave, I threw my good leg over the edge and rolled onto the top. I lay there panting, not caring who heard me.

I knew I would not be able to stand, so I rolled onto my hands and knees again and started crawling along the edge of the creek bank in the direction of the path, carefully holding my ankle up. The thin fabric of my running pants was totally shredded at the knees, but at least the pain of flesh getting rubbed raw distracted me from my ankle. I could just make out the path ahead of me. I stopped and listened, but could hear no sound other than my own breathing. Maybe they were gone.

I was probably the equivalent distance of a regular city block into the woods. Normally that would have been covered in a few minutes, but now it stretched in front of me like a marathon course.

I stopped and looked at my wristwatch. Like most runners' watches, mine had every feature known to man, including a light. It was 6:30. Then I remembered. Frank was coming to pick me up before six. Oh, my God. He must be panicking.

I took a deep breath and resumed my torturous crawl toward the road, willing myself to keep going. *Slow and steady wins the race,* I reminded myself. *Remember the tortoise.*

There was a little bend in the path, and as I came around, I could see lights flashing and hear voices. Frank's voice drowned out all the rest. "Goddammit, Clarence, do something. Get the searchlights. We have to find her. Who knows what those bastards have done with her."

I stopped my crawling and started screaming at the top of my lungs. "Frank, help! In the woods! I'm on the path!" Over and over I screamed his name. And like the time when I was ten and he was twelve, he came to the rescue. That time I had gotten my foot caught in a snag in the pond where we were forbidden to swim. We never told.

Frank came charging down the path, almost tripping over me. "What in the hell happened?" he asked as he leaned over and picked me up.

"They tried to run me over and then they tried to shoot me, so I ran, but I twisted my ankle real bad and couldn't get away, so I hid. Then I fell in the creek and hit my head and knocked myself out, but when I woke up I couldn't walk so I had to crawl. Oh, Frank, I was so scared."

"That's all right, Cousin, you're safe now. Just slow down. Who's they?"

"I didn't see them, but I know one was William, Reverend Smythe's driver, and the other one was Sheldon Junior. I don't know why Sheldon would want to hurt me. They were driving a big black car with tinted windows." I stopped and gasped, "Oh, my God. He didn't want to hurt me. He wanted me dead."

"You can't be serious," Frank said.

"I am, but the why is what I can't explain."

"You say they were in a big black car?"

"Yes, that's what they were driving when they tried to run me over."

"I saw that car," Frank said. "It was parked just up the road between our houses. I couldn't see who was in it because of the tinted windows."

"Sheldon was in the car. William was wandering around in the woods with his gun and flashlight, trying to find me. He must have gotten spooked when he saw you pull into my drive and called William off. They had arranged to stay in touch by their cell phones." I shook my head. "Why, Frank? Why?"

Even as I asked the question, a picture flashed through my mind and everything began to clear up. Reverend Smythe, Patricia and Sheldon, Junior, together at the reception. The reverend giving Patricia a big hug and kiss. Sheldon looking on with a mixture of longing and hate on his face. It was now clear to me. Sheldon wasn't jealous of the reverend. He was jealous of Patricia. Sheldon wanted to be the one in John Smythe's embrace. Poor Patricia. That's what she meant when she said, "Before I could pretend. Now he's made it real." Emily had it right. *You Can't Judge a Book by Its Cover.*

Sheldon and the reverend must have planned this whole thing to get control of Mr. Kroner's money. The bequest was in the reverend's name, not the church. Maybe they planned to split with the money and start a new life together. Poor Patricia was the dupe, nothing more. I became a threat when I began asking questions about the relationship between the two men and when I asked William where his sling was. Sheldon must have assumed I knew more than I did. It was all too complicated to explain to Frank. I'd wait till Gil got back.

"Frank, I'm cold and I hurt. Let's get out of here," I said

"Come on," Frank said and hoisted me over his shoulder. "Let's get you to the ER and get that ankle taken care of. Clarence," he yelled over his other shoulder, "Jessie says it was Sheldon Junior and someone named William and they are driving a big black sedan with tinted windows. Better call the state police. And after that, call the Sheriff and tell him to get his ass home."

Chapter 27

Gil was back in town and on his way over. He planned to stop and get a pizza for dinner. He even agreed to forgo the anchovies in lieu of my delicate condition.

It had been late by the time Frank and I got out of the emergency room. My worst fears had not materialized. My ankle was not broken, just badly sprained. The doctor had wrapped it, ordered me to stay off it, handed me a pair of crutches, told me to ice it, twenty minutes on, twenty minutes off, and made an appointment for me to come back in a week.

So here I sat. Foot up, ice bag on, waiting for Gil. Frank and Mildred and Aunt Henrietta had been in and out of the house all day, bearing gifts of food liberally laced with advice. Genevieve could not understand why I didn't want her on my lap, so she sulked on another chair.

Frank had filled me in on what happened when he found I wasn't home.

"I panicked when I discovered the house dark and you missing. I immediately assumed you had gone running and one of the local yokels had run you down. I had my cell with me, so I called 911. The operator kept me on the phone while she checked with the hospital, but, of course, you weren't there. So my next assumption was that you were dead or dying in a ditch somewhere. The operator said she would send Clarence out right away. You pretty much know the rest."

"You must have scared them away, thank heavens."

"I guess. It wasn't until Clarence arrived that we noticed the mailbox and newspaper holder had been demolished and mail scattered all over the place. Then I found a scrap of that gray shiny stuff your running outfit is made of on a bush about ten feet from the road. That was when I went ballistic. Well, you heard me."

"And a sweeter sound I have never heard. Thank you, Cousin."

Frank had wanted to take me to his house, but I had insisted on going home. I did let him get me upstairs to my bedroom and bring me water and a pain pill. Now I was waiting for Gil and the rest of the story.

I heard the Jeep pull in and hopped over to the door and let him inside. He dropped the pizza on the table and wrapped his arms around me.

"Dammit, Jessie, I thought I told you not to get involved? Do I have to lock you up to keep you safe? You're like a lightning rod, except instead of attracting electrical storms, you attract all the twisted, malevolent souls who live in or wander through Spencer County."

I couldn't answer him because he was squeezing me so hard. I balanced on my good leg and slowly peeled his arms loose.

"What kind of pizza did you bring me?"

"The deluxe with extra mushrooms on thin crust, what else?"

"Good. Now, please, help me back to my chair."

"Yes, ma'am. Anything else?"

"Two things. A martini and the rest of the story, as you know it."

Gil brought me my drink. I knew it would be perfect even before I tasted it. Tanquerey gin with a twist of lemon and a whisper of vermouth over lots of ice. James Bond might not have approved, but I thought it the best.

"I'm so sorry about your friend, Greg. Was it a nice service?"

"Jurisdictions from all over the State of Illinois sent representatives, the procession had to be a mile long, and the bagpipers were there. Yes, it was nice. They caught the guys who did it. A couple of punks. Left their fingerprints all over the place."

"Again, I'm sorry."

"Thanks. Knowing I had you to come back to made it easier for me. It was a good thing I didn't know you'd gotten yourself in the middle of a mess or Lord knows, what I would have done. Now, do you want to hear the rest of the escapade?"

"Have they caught William and Sheldon?"

"The State Police caught up with William about halfway between Springfield and Chicago, but there was no sign of Sheldon. Clarence checked with Patricia and Sheldon Senior, and they hadn't seen him or heard from him since lunch yesterday. They gave Clarence the license number. That's how the police got William so quickly. My gut tells me Sheldon Junior's not with us anymore."

"Do you think William killed him? Why would he do that?"

"William is known as Willy the Torch, and the rap sheet would curl your toes. He's been in and out of the penitentiary twice. If he's convicted again, it will be strike three and he's out. The M.O. on the arson at Kroner's matches his technique. Respect for human life doesn't rank high on William's resumé."

"What about the reverend? Did he hire William, knowing his background? Do you think he was part of the whole plot? What about his relationship with Sheldon?"

"Whoa. Let's take one question at a time. I better put the pizza in the oven to keep in warm. I have a feeling we won't eat till you're satisfied with my answers."

I watched as Gil propped the lid open slightly and slid the pizza box into the oven.

"About the reverend, we're not sure yet of the details of his part in the whole affair, though I'd bet he was in on it from the beginning. Our hope is that we can get William to spill all in exchange for assignment to a better prison facility, including how long he had worked for the reverend. Whether he will tell us what happened to Sheldon is another matter. Now I have a question for you."

"Okay. What?"

"When did you tumble on to the relationship between Sheldon and the reverend and how?"

I described the scene I had witnessed at the reception, Patricia's comments later, and my revelation in the woods. "Am I correct? Are they lovers?"

Gil nodded. "Patricia broke down when Clarence talked to her. She claims she didn't know for sure until a couple of days ago when she and Sheldon had a big argument and he blurted it out. He and the reverend met when he was in college. Sheldon was on the board for God's Fellowship so that gave him a reason to go to Chicago regularly."

"What about Ruby Holliday?"

"Again, it will take time to prove our theory, but she was probably hired by the reverend or Sheldon or both to impersonate the niece, with an eye to squeezing as much money out of Fred Kroner as possible. She may have tried a little blackmail after the plan fell through, so they had William dispose of her and torch the Kroner homestead. The old man set this whole thing in motion when he made a new will and then died."

"So you think the same thing happened with Floyd?"

"Yep. I'll bet the tox screen shows that something got slipped into his drink at Smitty's."

"What about the money?"

Gil shrugged. "Who knows? That will be up to the lawyers, after we get this whole thing figured out and proven. If the reverend is guilty, he can't inherit. Could be it will go to the two hated Kroner brothers. Wouldn't that be ironic? Now, can we eat? I'm starving. And by the way, the next time I have to go out of town, I'm taking you with me. Plan on it. It's not safe to leave you behind in Riverport."

ABOUT THE AUTHOR

Janet Majerus grew up in Quincy, Illinois, on the bluffs overlooking the Mississippi River. Her first book was *Grandpa and Frank,* which was made into a TV movie *Home to Stay,* starring Henry Fonda. She left writing for a career in politics in University City, Missouri, a suburb of St. Louis where she was elected first to the city council and then as mayor. After she retired from public service, she started writing again. This is her second mystery starring Jessie Schroeder. The first was *The Best Laid Plans.* She and her husband Robert Burke now live outside of Taos in northern New Mexico.